THE TRIBULATIONS OF
ELEANOR MARCH

Also by Michael J. McCann

Michael J. McCann

The Plaid Raccoon Press

The Tribulations of Eleanor March

A MARCH AND WALKER CRIME NOVEL

ISBN: 978-1-927884- 36-2 (paperback)
eBook ISBN: 978-1-927884- 37-9 (e-book)

Front cover image: perspicacious_esthete from Pixabay
Back cover image: Stockcake
Internal images: Stockcake; Pixabay (public domain)
Author photo: © 2025 by Michael J. McCann

Visit the author's website at www.mjmccann.com

To John and Bev Carr,
with love and thanks for
all your support.

PRESENT DAY

CHAPTER 1

Ontario Provincial Police Detective Inspector Ellie March was tired.

It was the end of a long day. As she drove out of the parking lot of the OPP Lanark detachment office on Dufferin Street in Perth, she realized she hadn't eaten anything since the night before. A chicken salad sandwich, she thought. She wasn't sure.

She was starving.

She drove a block and a half to the McDonald's and waited in the Drive-Thru line to place her order.

Her eyes slowly closed. Unfortunately, though, she could still see the photographs of the case she and the crime unit had worked since dawn yesterday morning. A young female living in Lanark village, in her late teens. Sexually assaulted by an uncle who'd been passed out on the couch all night. A brutal attack, with horrific injuries. A detailed statement from the victim's younger sister, who'd driven her to the hospital, where the police were called.

In the province of Ontario, sexual assault is deemed a major case occurrence, meaning that Ellie March assumed command of the investigation as a major case manager, overseeing the detectives of the Lanark County Crime Unit and the regional forensic identification officers as they gathered evidence and interrogated the suspect.

It had taken all day yesterday for the victim to be examined, treated, and interviewed at the hospital. A traumatic experience at the best of times. It had also taken hours for the warrants to be issued and the physical evidence gathered at the scene, and more hours, stretching into late last night, for everything to be processed and analyzed at the regional lab in Smiths Falls. It had also taken more than a day for the suspect to finally cave in to questioning and admit what he had done.

At that point Ellie's focus doubled down in earnest as she guided the team through the detail-oriented process of assembling the case that would be handed to the assistant Crown Attorney for prosecution. All their hard work would be gathered up into what was known as a Report to Crown Counsel, or a Crown Brief, in which the accusations against the suspect, the evidence sustaining these accusations, witnesses who were interviewed and their statements, and the procedures followed to bring charges were all carefully set out in an organized and complete statement of the facts.

It was a detail-oriented business, and yet it had to be

simple and logical—

"May I take your order, please? Hello?"

Ellie crawled back into present tense and leaned out her open window. "Five Big Macs."

"Would you like fries and a soft drink with that?"

"No."

She paid at the next window and rolled forward, next in line to exit back onto Dufferin. Two of the burgers were hers and the other three were for Reggie, her bear of a German Shepherd. She'd eat one of hers and put the other in the fridge for later. Reggie would scarf down all three of his right away and—

She pulled out onto the street and hit the brakes as a car changed lanes right in front of her and smacked into her Tahoe. Belatedly the front-collision alert began to emit high-pitched beeps as her head snapped forward. By the time it stopped, she had collected herself enough to realize that she wasn't hurt. Two men were getting out of the other car, so she got out as well.

"You didn't signal your lane change," she said as they advanced on her.

The driver, small and greasy looking, ran a hand through his rat-chewed hair. The other, tall and heavy, wore a black London Fog raincoat despite the heat, black jeans, a black T-shirt, and Ray-Ban Wayfarer-style sunglasses.

She glanced at the front of her car. The Tahoe was her newly issued motor pool vehicle, replacing the Crown Victoria she'd driven for so long it had felt like a second home to her. She missed it, but not enough to prevent her from falling in love with the Tahoe. It was big, powerful, and nearly new, with much more comfort and electronic functionality than she'd had before with the Crown Vic. Now here it was with a smashed headlight and damage to the bumper and front fender.

The car that had hit her, a vintage-looking black Thunderbird, had similar damage—

"Stupid bitch."

Frowning, she looked at the driver. Baring his teeth, he punched her in the stomach. Air whooshed from her and she folded over, just in time to meet an uppercut that caught her under the chin and flipped her over onto the pavement.

Down and out.

CHAPTER 2

Ontario Provincial Police Detective Constable Kevin Walker opened the front door of the Victorian red brick house on Drummond Street East in Perth and stepped into the hallway, closing the door behind him.

On the left was a staircase, at the bottom of which was a sign on the wall. Featuring an old-fashioned arrow pointing upstairs, the sign declared that the floor above was occupied by "Nicholas Rush Investigations." On the right was a doorway and another sign, this one identifying the downstairs as the domain of The Jane Walker Salon.

He stepped into a smallish room that had once been the front parlour of the house and was now a very posh and stylishly furnished welcoming room. A young redhead sat behind an Edwardian oak reception desk that had once belonged to the Queen's Hotel on Foster Street. The redhead, whose name was Fiadh Murphy (her name was pronounced *Fee*-ah) was anything but Edwardian, but her modest black dress matched the tone of the room, as did the smile she gave Kevin.

"Hi. She's just in the back."

"Here I am," Janie said, putting her hand on his arm to turn him around.

He bent down and kissed her. She squeezed his bicep.

He handed her a lunch bag. "Here you go."

The bag was black with two leather handles and a zipper. It had a large "J" on the side and two white roses. Her son Brendan had bought it for her as a birthday gift last September, and this morning she'd forgotten it on the kitchen counter when she'd hurried off to work.

"Thanks, champ. You're wearing your hat."

Kevin grinned, settling it on his head self-consciously. "Sure. It's my new look."

"I think it's great. Fee, what do you think?"

"Definitely grand," the redhead replied, being the soul of diplomacy.

Janie had bought it for him as a Father's Day gift. He found a place for it in the hall closet, far enough back on the shelf that she couldn't see it without the use of a step stool, being the short person that she was, but eventually she'd caught up to him. When she asked what was wrong with it, he hemmed and hawed before finally admitting there was nothing wrong with it. Yes, it fit. Yes, it was stylish. Yes, he would wear it. Starting tomorrow.

As headwear went, it was pretty harmless. A newsboy's

cap, charcoal grey, made of Donegal tweed, it was the kind that was constructed of eight panels joined at the crown with a button. It had a blunt bill and a bit of shape to it, unlike a driver's cap or so-called flat cap, which looked like it needed to be removed with a bottle opener.

She'd paid more than a hundred dollars for it online, plus shipping from Ireland, so he damned well better wear it.

She winked and took her lunch bag into the back room to toss into the mini-fridge she kept there for staff lunches, cans of pop, and other necessities.

Kevin heard the stairs creaking and he backed up a few steps so that he could see out into the hallway.

Nick Rush stood at the bottom of the stairs. He gave Kevin a nod and a little crook of his finger.

Kevin looked back at Janie, who was talking to a customer while one of her hairdressers fiddled in a mass of brown hair with the long pointed end of a comb. He smiled at the redhead behind the Edwardian leviathan and followed Nick upstairs.

The reception area of Nicholas Rush Investigations consisted of a waiting space (coffee table covered with old magazines; mismatched chairs; a side table with a snake plant on it); gunmetal grey filing cabinets (government surplus); and a desk that usually featured Nick's assistant, Luke Ferguson (former biker and scary dude). The desk was currently unoccupied.

Nick led the way into his private office and sat down behind his file-strewn desk. Kevin eased into a visitor's chair and crossed his legs.

"Nice hat."

"Thanks."

"I wonder if you'd do me favour."

"Sure, Nick. If I can. What would you like?"

Nick leaned back and crossed his arms. He was the kind of guy you'd walk right past on the sidewalk without a glance on a typical Monday morning. He was medium height, about five-ten, with a slightly heavy build. Somewhere in his forties, he looked like a high school shop teacher or the guy you'd see stocking shelves in the Canadian Tire. His mousy brown hair was trimmed short and receding at the temples. His glasses had thick, black frames.

The perfect look for a private investigator.

The nameplate on his desk said "N.O. Rush." No Rush. It was Nick's nickname, as it were, a convenient contraction of Nicholas Oliver Rush. A joke, but not really. Nick never rushed. He took his time, did everything carefully, and handed his clients the results.

Nick owned the building in which they were currently sitting, and therefore he was Janie's landlord. As such, he was her dream come true. He left her to run her business and didn't interfere. Her slightest wish was his desire. Problems were fixed as soon as she pointed them out. Since he used her rent to pay the taxes on the property, which had gone up like everything else over the years, the extra outlay for maintenance and upkeep stressed him not in the slightest. The mortgage had been paid off several years ago after a particularly lucrative contract had come through with a very handsome fee, and so Nick was a reasonably happy man, as far as his place of business was concerned.

"You may have noticed," Nick began, "that Luke's not here today. He called in asking for a day off, which is not like him. We talked for a while."

Kevin waited. Luke was about ten years older than his boss, a former member of the Outlaws Motorcycle Club who'd retired after a serious traffic accident. He found work with a security company and wandered into Nick's span of attention during a case. Nick quickly offered him a job at twice what he was making as a parking lot flag man and night watchman, and Luke didn't hesitate.

"He's upset because a good friend of his had something valuable stolen from him. The friend asked Luke to help him out, since Luke's now a P.I. kind of guy."

Kevin smiled, knowing Luke wasn't licenced to operate as a private investigator, as Nick was, but he was a nosey parker nonetheless and liked to find out stuff. Nick had offered once to help him prepare for the exam to get his certification, but Luke had turned him down. He harboured a deep-seated suspicion of authority that wouldn't allow him to knuckle under to some government toad in exchange for a piece of paper and a laminated card.

"So what's the favour?" Kevin asked. "Do you want me to look into this theft he's interested in?"

"It's an outboard boat motor. Apparently an expensive one. I don't know anything about it, and the guy can't afford me, and I don't work pro bono."

"Has it been reported to the police?"

"Apparently the guy's more allergic to the cops than Luke is, if that's even possible."

"So he won't want me showing up, Nick. I don't get it."

"Luke asked me to ask you. As a favour. That's all I know about it."

Kevin sighed. Nick wasn't the only one who didn't provide pro bono services. If it was a case of theft, particularly one where the property had a value over $5,000, it was an indictable offence and needed to be brought to the official attention of the crime unit for investigation.

"Where do I find these goobers?"

Nick recited Luke's address. "I'll tell them you're coming."

"Sure," Kevin said. "Thanks."

CHAPTER 3

Kevin found Detective Constable Liam Woolfson in the lunch room, drinking black tea from a cup and saucer while reading the news on his cellphone.

"Morning, Kevin," he said, glancing at him over the rim of his teacup. "How goes the battle?"

"It's tough, but I do believe we're winning. And you?"

"Lovely. Raring to go." Liam had been with the detachment for a little more than two months and was still getting settled in. To say that he was a character with a quirky personality and baggage to go with it would be a gross understatement. He'd transferred into Lanark from North Bay after having been cleared of an excessive use of force complaint. It had been filed after his arrest of a notorious Indian Posse member who'd moved from Winnipeg to set up shop in the Bay. The investigation found that Liam had engaged in fisticuffs with the guy, but in self-defence, as substantiated by several eye witnesses who took their lives in their hands, literally, to come forward. Liam was absolved of wrongdoing, and a subsequent civil law suit quickly failed, but a transfer out of the region was deemed to be the prudent thing to do.

The Lanark detachment had experienced a series of changes during the year. Detective Constable Doug Skelton had resigned, creating an opening for Liam. Skelton was now enrolled in the Canada Pension Plan Disability Benefit program, an income replacement system for people under sixty-five who have to quit working because of a disability. In Skelton's case, he was fighting liver cancer, and the prognosis wasn't good. Heather Hope had moved over from working with Kevin to handle Skelton's case load in property crimes.

Meanwhile, Detective Constable Bob Pierce, "The Actor," had transferred up to the Orillia detachment, where he was being groomed by the Powers That Be for a future assignment in General Headquarters. A rising star in the force, to be sure.

Detective Sergeant Sonja Freeling still commanded the crime unit, and Detective Constable Alaric Quinn, her friend, remained in Lanark as their lead investigator for cybercrime and intelligence-led policing, so there was some continuity in the unit. Along with the addition of Liam, though, Inspector Colleen Galvin, the detachment commander, had brought in a young and serious-minded detective constable named Aydin Farzan, who transferred from Middlesex at the same time as Liam made the move from North Bay.

Kevin watched Liam rinse out his cup and saucer and leave them upside down on a tea towel to dry. The jury was still out on the man. He was clearly a flake, but all the signs pointed to a reliable cop with enough moxie to get the job done. Time would tell.

Luke Ferguson lived in a three-storey apartment building on Wilson Street, four blocks away from the detachment office. He opened the door at Kevin's knock and stepped aside. He wiped his hand on his jeans and shook Kevin's hand.

"Sorry, just rebuilding a carb. Come on in."

Luke was a few inches shorter than Kevin, who stood six-four and weighed 250 pounds, and was about a decade older. His handlebar moustache was iron grey, as was his short-cropped hair, and his face bore scars on his left temple, his chin, and at the right corner of his mouth. He was missing an earlobe.

"This is Detective Constable Woolfson," Kevin said.

Luke and Liam exchanged looks.

The balcony door slid open.

"This is Gerry Millen," Luke said.

Millen nodded and sat down at the kitchen table. He was in his mid-thirties, a skinny redhead in a black sleeveless T-shirt with the Guns N Roses logo on it. Both arms bore tattoo sleeves featuring roses; someone's portrait; a roaring tiger; trailing ivy; a coiled snake around his right wrist and skeletal bones on his fingers. On the back of his left hand was an open eye, and on the back of each finger at the proximal phalange, where they'd be visible when he made a fist—which he was doing right now—were the logos of Superman, Batman, Green Lantern, and The Flash.

"Whose carburetor?" Kevin asked.

Luke sat down and picked up a part. The carburetor looked old and a little the worse for wear. Its pieces were scattered across a newspaper spread out on the table to protect it from grease and dirt, of which there seemed to be quite a bit.

"Mine," Millen said. "Off a Honda CB750 I picked up for my sister. She's into bikes."

"Good kid," Luke offered, wiping the part with an oily rag.

"The Hornet or the Nighthawk?" Liam asked.

No one answered.

Kevin sat down across from Luke. "Tell me about the outboard motor."

Luke glanced at Millen, who folded his arms defensively. "It's a '22 Merc 115. Four-stroke; electric start. Retailed at fourteen-point-nine K but I paid eleven."

"It's for his dad," Luke said, selecting another part and squinting at it.

Kevin raised his eyebrows.

"For his sixty-fifth birthday. He's retiring. He's a big fisherman and has a boat at our cottage on the lake—Mississippi—but the motor he's got is a cheap piece of shit and I decided he deserved an upgrade."

"Which the Merc is," Luke said. "Great for trolling,

with lots of power and fuel efficiency like you wouldn't believe. I went to look at it with him."

"Where'd you get it?"

"Off a guy up in Lanark. Has an engine repair shop up there."

"Name of?"

"Partridge. Howard or something."

"Hollis," Kevin said. He knew the man from previous interactions with stolen property, including a chain saw that had belonged to a murder victim, Grant Burnham. Partridge promptly reported suspicious equipment whenever he encountered it. He was an honest and reliable dealer. "So tell me what happened."

"I brought it up to the cottage and locked it in a tool shed. Left it there three, four days. When I took Dad up to give it to him, someone had cut the padlock, looks like with a bolt cutter, and it was gone."

"Who knew it was there?"

"Nobody. Well, me and my brother. That's it."

"What's your brother's name?"

"Harry."

Kevin glanced at Liam, who was taking notes. "How'd you get eleven grand to buy it?"

Millen rolled his eyes. "I sold my wife's Tesla. She got a second DUI and won't be driving for a while, so there was no sense letting it sit around losing value."

"I see. What'd you get for it?"

"Thirty-six."

"Nice. You wouldn't have a picture of the motor, would

you?"

Millen lifted a haunch and pulled out his cellphone. After a few swipes and taps, he handed it to Kevin. A black outboard motor, all right. The Mercury name was displayed in white lettering across the powerhead, and the propeller was made of shiny stainless steel.

"There's another one. Just swipe."

Kevin swiped. The next photograph showed the identification plate, where the serial number of the motor was printed. He tipped the phone so that Liam could jot down the particulars, then he handed it back to Millen.

"Send them to me, will you?"

"Sure. Where?"

Kevin recited the general inquiries e-mail address for the detachment. They waited while Millen sent them off.

"Thanks," he said, somewhat mollified that Kevin seemed to be taking it seriously.

Kevin and Liam stood and went to the door. "Just leave it with us for a couple of days, all right?"

In the hallway, someone came out of their apartment a few doors down as Kevin gave Luke a stern look. "No charging around breaking heads and trashing people's garages. We'll look into it."

Luke rolled his eyes.

"While you're at it," the guy down the hallway said, "could you see if they've made any progress finding my car?"

Luke gave Kevin a quick salute and closed the door.

"You're with the police, right?" the neighbour asked.

"Yes, sir."

"I don't understand why you guys can't do anything right. It's been two weeks now and I haven't heard a damned thing from you. Do you have any idea how much I've got tied up in that thing? The insurance company's being a shit, and I've just about had it up to here with all the wall-to-wall incompetence."

Kevin walked down to him. "What's your name, sir?"

"Chris King. It's right there in the report I filed *two weeks ago.*"

"Personally, we haven't seen the file, since someone else is working it, but I tell you what. Let's step inside and you can fill us in on the details."

King threw up his hands. "Again? Why not. I don't have anything better to do."

As he turned away and opened his apartment door, Kevin glanced at Liam, who grinned and shook his head.

CHAPTER 4

Ellie woke up and found herself chained to a cot in a small room. She lay there for a long while, trying to put the pieces together. A black Thunderbird. Riding in the back seat of a hearse. A rat-faced guy. Her jaw ached and her stomach was sore.

She managed to get up on one elbow to look around.

The room was about twelve by twelve. No windows. One door. An old metal government surplus desk had been shoved against the far wall. It was covered with piles of factory repair and service manuals for various cars and trucks, along with after-market volumes from Chilton and Haynes. In front of it was an office chair on wheels. She looked at grey, four-drawer filing cabinets; an old cork board covered with dusty memos and other documents; and a whiteboard on wheels. In the top corner of the whiteboard, someone had taped a brief message: "Do Not Write on This Board!" Underneath it, on the board, someone had written "Okay."

There were cardboard boxes of empty oil cans; a metal rack holding old electric typewriters, Rolodexes, and telephone answering machines; and a wooden stool.

It was a junk room. They'd chained her to an army-issue metal cot in a junk room.

Her bladder began to give her grief. She called out, but it was little more than a croak. The cot was bolted to the floor, but there was enough slack in the chain that she could bang it against the leg, metal on metal. Click, click, click.

She gathered her strength and banged harder.

Clang, clang, clang.

After a while, the door opened.

"Toilet," she managed.

The door closed. Eventually it opened again, and a woman came in. She was short, Black, and grim-faced. She unlocked Ellie's chain, helped her to her feet, and led her out into a wood-panelled corridor. They shuffled down to a door with the familiar pictogram indicating a female washroom. The woman helped Ellie into a stall and held the door open as Ellie relieved herself.

When she was done, the woman took her back to the room, chained her up again, and left. A man stood in the doorway, looking at her.

"Where am I?" Ellie asked.

"In trouble, that's where you are." He was short, of

mixed race, with a black beard and dreadlocks that hung down his back. His eyes were large and brown.

Light-headedness swept her down onto the cot. Had they given her something to knock her out? She was vaguely aware of the man closing the door as she drifted into unconsciousness.

CHAPTER 5

The following morning, which was Wednesday, Kevin tried to reach Ellie on the phone, but it rang through six times before being forwarded to voicemail. He stewed about it while he went through his e-mail Inbox and filed away a few paper documents lying around on his desk, then he made up his mind and slipped on his jacket and hat.

"Back in about an hour," he said, sticking his head into Sonja's office.

On the way, he tried calling again, but with the same result. He wondered what was going on. As a major case manager, Ellie reported to the director of the Criminal Investigations Branch at General Headquarters in Orillia. A different bureaucratic stovepipe from the regional organization in which Kevin, the crime unit, and the rest of the detachment were situated. It was entirely possible that she'd been called up to GHQ for some reason and hadn't bothered to mention it. She didn't particularly owe the detachment or the region an accounting of her whereabouts at any given time.

Still, it didn't sit right with Kevin. He'd never known her to be inaccessible like this before.

Although she reported to Orillia, Ellie lived in a four-season cottage on Sparrow Lake, around sixty kilometers south of Perth. It gave her a somewhat more centralized access to her territorial responsibilities, which covered most of East Region, including the Lanark County detachment. When she'd first decided to move into the area, Kevin had helped her line up the purchase with the owner, Gerry Staley, a goaltending coach with the University of Victoria and a former draft choice of the Nashville Predators. Kevin gave her a hand moving in, and they'd become friends as well as fellow service members.

He arrived at the cottage and saw that her vehicle was gone. He got out and walked down the slope to the building.

It was a nice, well-kept place. It had originally come with two bedrooms, but Ellie had converted one of them into her office and added an extension with floor-to-ceiling shelves that she kept stocked with bottled water, canned goods, batteries, emergency supplies, and other such necessities. It wasn't that she was a survivalist, exactly—it was just that she believed in redundancy.

He followed the path around the extension and tried the kitchen door. Locked.

He could hear Reggie inside, barking. He looked

through the window. Reggie's food bowl was overturned and the water dish was empty.

Several years ago, Ellie had entrusted to him the keypad and alarm codes in case of emergency. He'd memorized them rather than write them down somewhere. He let himself in, and Reggie banged against his leg as he ran outside. Kevin watched as the dog abruptly stopped at a tree for a long pee, after which he began to hunt around for a good spot to defecate. Reggie and he were friends, and the dog would come back inside when Kevin suggested it was time. Theoretically.

He filled Reggie's bowls and took a quick look around. He saw nothing out of the ordinary, and nothing that would suggest where Ellie might have gone. The air carried the faint odours of coffee and dog.

He reset the alarm and opened the kitchen door. Reggie was not in sight. Kevin whistled, and the dog stuck his head out from behind a large cedar tree.

"Come on in, big boy."

Reggie ducked back, then reluctantly trotted over and bumped past Kevin into the kitchen.

"She'll be home soon," Kevin said. "Just hang on a bit. Eat some puppy chow and have a snooze."

Reggie sniffed at the kibble in his bowl and dug in.

Kevin locked the door behind him and drove to the detachment office.

Sonja Freeling was sitting at her desk, rubbing lotion into her hands. Her straight, blond hair was pulled back into a ponytail, and her blue-framed glasses were perched on the end of her nose. She glanced up over them and smiled.

"Nice hat."

"Thanks. Have you heard anything from Ellie lately?"

She shook her head. "She's not upstairs?"

The detachment building had a second floor where an office had been set aside for Ellie's use whenever she was managing a major case in Lanark.

"No. And not at home."

"You went to check on her."

He nodded.

"Why, are you worried?"

Kevin shrugged, biting his lip. "I don't know. A gut feeling. Something's not right."

"Maybe it's her father, and she had to go to Toronto on short notice."

"Would you mind making a call or two? Maybe Colleen could call her boss at GHQ."

"Sure."

"If it's all right with you, Liam and I are going to give Heather a hand with some of her stolen car files."

"Thanks, Kevin." She squirted more lotion into her palm. "I was working on the Corvette last night. Had to scrub like the devil afterwards. Now my hands are all chapped."

"How's it coming?"

She grinned. "Oh, it's ready to roll. Took it for a spin this morning before work. God, I love Corvettes. Candy apple red, Kevin. A jewel."

Heather Hope from Keene was in her cubicle, frowning at her computer monitor. Liam sat down in her visitor's chair, and Kevin leaned on the doorframe.

"Got a sec? Liam and I have been poaching on a case of yours."

She threw herself back in her chair, making it creak with the effort. "Feel free, Kev. I hate property. I *hate* it. These case files are a mess. Did Skelton spend any time on them at all, or was he too busy playing 'Mary had a little lamb'?"

"Now, now, Heather. Let's not speak ill of the, uh, ill."

Heather glared at him. She wore one of her favourite T-shirts—red, a little tight, and featuring a hammer and the slogan "This is not a drill!" Her dark hair was pinned back in an old-fashioned bun, and a polka-dotted handkerchief stuck out of a pocket of her knee-length, 1950s-style, yellow wrap-around skirt.

"Liam and I talked to Chris King yesterday."

"Who the hang is he?"

Kevin smiled despite himself. "One of your clients, detective. Auto theft. A white 2022 Lexus RX 350."

"King." She tapped on her keyboard and scrolled with her mouse until she had the file open. "Okay. Here it is. Haven't looked at it yet."

Heather had great peripheral vision, and she caught Liam's glance at Kevin. "I'll have you know," she growled, "I've been working around the clock just trying to figure out his B-and-Es."

Liam held up a hand. "I didn't say a word."

"I told Sonja we can give you a hand, if you want," Kevin said.

"I want. On the car thefts?"

"That's what I'm thinking."

"That would be great, Kev. I appreciate it."

Sitting next to her monitor was a six-inch-tall Tweety Bird. It had a plastic body and a rubber head with a pinhole in the top. Liam picked it up and squeezed the head, producing a loud squeak.

"Stop that," Heather said.

He put it down. "Hey Heather, why did Tweety Bird go to the hospital?"

She rolled her eyes.

"Because she needed tweetment. What's the strongest bird? A crane. What do you call a bird that's afraid of heights? A chicken." He grinned. "Sorry, I'm just winging it today. I'll be here all week."

Exuding disdain, Heather ran a query on stolen vehicles in Lanark County for the year to date and came up with sixty-six hits. "Holy crap."

Alaric Quinn strolled in, scratching his beard. "Over fifteen thousand vehicles were stolen last year in Ontario between January to June. I don't know what the numbers are so far this year, but I don't think they've dropped off by very much."

"Heather," Kevin said, "could you run a query by book value? Say, everything in the county over fifty K?"

She did so, and pointed at the screen. "Twenty-four. That seems to me like a lot in just over six months. Like, one a week, for crying out loud."

"I'm curious," Kevin said. "Break it down by municipality."

She did so. "Twelve in Carleton Place; eight in Perth; two in Mississippi Mills; and two in Almonte."

Alaric grunted. "Some kind of organized activity targeting high-end vehicles. Wouldn't you say, Kevin?"

"Looks like."

"Would you like me to give you a hand with this?" Alaric asked Heather. "I could do some analysis and pull together a report."

"That'd be great. Meanwhile, these two birds have volunteered to do some field work for me."

"What do you call two crows in a field?" Liam asked her. "An attempted murder."

"I wish you wouldn't keep setting him up with straight lines," Kevin complained.

Liam's grin filled the cubicle.

CHAPTER 6

That evening, the man with the long dreadlocks and goatee brought Ellie her supper. It was a pie plate filled with baked beans, a piece of toast, and a couple of sliced-up hotdogs.

"It's the best I could do," he said, pulling up a stool and sitting down just inside the door. "Everybody else went home, and this was all I could find."

"It's all right." Ellie dug in, starving. They hadn't fed her lunch, and she'd been worried they'd skip this meal as well. She was an omnivore in the true sense of the word: she'd eat pretty much anything that found its way up to her end of the food chain.

"My name's Junior," he said. "Junior Paul. What's yours?"

"Eleanor. Eleanor March."

"I'm sorry we have to do this, Mrs. March. Squid and Andrew panicked. They should have just left you there, but they were afraid you'd be a witness. Which I guess you are."

Ellie shrugged, spooning up the last of the beans. For a crook, Junior seemed affable enough. Maybe he'd end up talking his way into a jail cell. In the meantime, it seemed prudent to establish some kind of alias to hide the fact that she was law enforcement.

"So what are you people doing here, Junior? What am I a witness to?"

"Better that you don't know. What about you?"

"I'm a housecleaner. Part time. I don't need much. My husband died two years ago, and I put the insurance money into a trust, so I make out okay. The mortgage is paid off on the house, so that's a big thing."

"Good for you."

"Tell me something, Junior. Who's that little weasel who hit me? Squid. What's the story on him?"

She was testing him, of course. Wanting to see how much he'd tell her. She'd try to work for information, nibble around the edges, see what she could get. It was a risk, given the time-honoured tradition of killing a kidnap victim once they've seen your face and learned too much. Oh well. As Captain Kirk once said, "Risk . . . is our business."

"He's from east Europe somewhere," Junior said. "Belarus, I think it is. Well, not him. His parents. Squid's from Toronto."

"Why Squid?"

Junior laughed. "I haven't a clue. Maybe because he looks like one. Don't ask me what his real name is."

"Have you known him long?"

"A few years. We all met in Montreal." Junior stood up. "Enough for now. Get some sleep, Eleanor. May I call you that? Or would you prefer Mrs. March?"

"Eleanor's fine," she said, lowering her head to the pillow. They were definitely putting something in her food. She felt herself drifting away.

CHAPTER 7

The following morning, which was Thursday, Kevin, Heather, and Liam sorted through the files in the lunch room, which was currently not in use.

Alaric wandered in and sat down. He was drinking some kind of green sludge from a promotional water bottle. He picked up a file and leafed through it.

"What the hell's that?" Heather demanded, staring at his bottle.

"Kratom."

"What the hell's that?"

"A supplement from southeast Asia. It's an analgesic, and it also helps with anxiety."

Liam frowned. "Isn't it illegal?"

"Pfhht. Not in Canada. In some states down in Wonderland, yeah, but it's perfectly legal up here. I broke my kneecap when I was in high school, and it aches like the devil on days like today, when it's hot and damp and there's rain coming."

"Does the stuff help?"

"Yep."

Kevin was skeptical, but he smiled when Liam leaned forward, squinting at the water bottle. He figured he knew what was coming.

"Neat," Liam said. "Where'd you get it?"

Alaric held the bottle out at arm's-length, admiring it. "Intel Twelfth Gen."

"What the hell's that?" Heather asked yet again.

"It refers to the twelfth generation of Intel Core processors, which were code named Alder Lake. They came out in October of 2021, succeeding Tiger Lake and Rock Lake."

"Well, that tells me a helluva lot."

"Where'd you get it?" Liam repeated.

"I found it in a cardboard box of freebies in a vendor's booth at the Consumer Electronics show in Vegas. January 2022."

"The artwork's pretty cool."

Alaric smiled. "Yeah. And you can't beat a freebie."

Liam said, "I know a guy who went to buy a dozen bees to start an apiary. The vendor gave him thirteen. The guy said, 'You over-counted' and the vendor said, 'Nah, that last one's a freebie.'"

"Jesus," Heather muttered. "I'm trying to read."

Liam was just getting started. "Electronics show, eh? Two antennas got married on a roof. The wedding was only so-so, but the reception was great."

Kevin had to smile.

"Why did the capacitor kiss the diode? He couldn't resistor."

Alaric said to Kevin, "Does this guy have an off switch?"

"What do electricians call a power outage? A current event."

Heather threw a paper clip at him.

"Sorry." Liam tried to swallow his grin and failed.

"Maybe I could summarize." Alaric took a swig of his green bilge and patted his lips with a tissue. "It might be helpful to start with thefts in Perth and the surrounding townships."

"Good idea," Kevin said.

Alaric pushed his glasses up on his forehead and rubbed his eyes. "Of the ten thefts, only four had a book value above fifty K. There was a 2020 Land Rover stolen from the owner's driveway last November; a 2022 Ford F-150 stolen from the town hall parking lot while the owner was inside paying a bunch of parking tickets and complaining about it; that one was in March; and a classic 1974 BMW 3.0 CSI, powder blue, stolen from a storage facility on the edge of town, also in March. Plus Chris King's 2022 Lexus RX 350."

"All very nice rides," Liam said.

"Each theft seems to be different." Alaric repositioned his glasses and blinked at Kevin. "Maybe something will turn up when you interview these people that will help us put together a more comprehensive picture of the group that's behind it all."

"Hopefully."

"One more thing." Alaric sucked at his drink. "Something they do that's part of a car theft operation is have what they call a cooling spot. When a high-end car's stolen, it's immediately driven to this cooling spot and hidden from sight for maybe a week or so. Once the search for it has cooled down enough for it to be moved, they'll put it in a container and haul it to a seaport where it's shipped overseas. They like the Port of Montreal, for example, and Africa and the Middle East are popular destinations."

"Sounds like a lot of money's involved," Liam said.

"You've got that right."

"So we should find this cooling spot, if it's around here. How do we do that?"

"Good old fashioned detective work," Heather said. "Like they pay us for. It's why our asses aren't stuck in a cruiser driving up and down Highway 7 all day."

"That could change in a flash," Sonja said from the doorway. "I checked for you, and the training room's now booked in your name for the next week. Get set up in there and let people drink their coffee in peace."

As they gathered up their stuff, Kevin said, "Let's get a map and take a good look at the layout of this thing."

CHAPTER 8

The next time that Ellie was given a trip to the washroom, it was Junior who accompanied her. Apparently the woman wasn't available this time around.

Initially, Ellie had wondered if she'd end up being sexually assaulted while they held her captive here. If one of these men took it in his head that she was an easy target of opportunity for a little extracurricular activity, there wasn't much that she would be able to do to protect herself. The sedatives they were obviously giving her were just as effective a restraint as their chains and locks, keeping her flat on her back and just this side of docile, so she knew she was vulnerable to attack.

However, no one had shown the slightest interest in her. Apparently with this bunch it was an advantage to be a plain-looking, middle aged woman with unattractive, shoulder-length hair and a flat bust. Or they were just too damned busy making money to give a crap.

As she walked beside Junior to the washroom, she wobbled a bit, the sedative causing her to be unsteady on her feet. Junior put his arm around her waist to guide her. The way a son would give his elderly mother a bit of help when she needed it.

Cripes.

Of course, because her mind was not completely within her control right now, she reflexively remembered walking her adoptive-mother Mary to the washroom in her assisted-living unit in Scarborough. It was 2019, and she'd driven down from Sparrow Lake for a visit, to see how she was doing. Paul had passed away two months before, and she knew that Mary was pining for him.

She was also contending with the middle stages of dementia herself, Mary was, and she didn't like to be helped. She cursed Ellie all the way into the bathroom, and when Ellie saw she didn't need any assistance getting settled on the toilet, she withdrew, leaving the door open a crack. She waited patiently until she heard the toilet flush, then opened the door and helped Mary wash her hands and get back into bed. No more cursing. She even thanked her.

Mary was dead a month later, from pneumonia.

When Paul had died, a close friend in the Polish community named Ludmila Abramowicz took care of all the arrangements for Mary. A lawyer, Jakub Dudek, was executor. The same two friends stepped forward when

Mary passed away, and so Ellie had little more to do once again other than be present as the sole survivor of their little family. It was all very sad.

Mary left almost nothing as an inheritance. They'd sold their Yonge Street business years ago, and the money had been mostly used up by the monthly payments for their assisted-living unit. Ellie instructed Ludmila to donate the clothing, knick-knacks, and other miscellaneous items to the local St. Vincent de Paul charity store. She told Dudek to donate the balance of the bank accounts on behalf of the estate to the Polish Association of Toronto.

Ludmila held back two items that Ellie could take home as her inheritance, if she wished. One was a lovely tea pot that a relative had managed to send over to Canada after Mary had settled here. It was the pot she always used to make tea every day for herself and Paul.

The other item was an old book that had been Paul's prized possession, a volume of poetry by Adam Mickiewicz entitled *Ballady i Romanse*, a well-worn edition published in Leipzig in 1852.

His father, Stanley Marchalewicz, had kept it shoved in the waistband of his trousers when he and his wife, Lena, and their two children fled Poland in 1944. In that year, a total of 12,800 Poles came to Canada, stateless and displaced persons in the aftermath of the war. They'd been politically active, participating in the Warsaw Uprising of August 1 of that year. A non-communist underground resistance army tried to take control of the city from the Germans before the Soviet Army arrived. The uprising went on for two months until the Germans finally levelled the city in October.

Stanley and Lena Marchalewicz were citizens who participated by supplying the insurgents, providing first aid, and other support. When it all fell apart, they were forced to flee. In transit, their eight-year-old daughter Natalia disappeared from their group. She was never found. In Canada, Stanley found work in Toronto as a city garbage worker. Paul entered Grade Seven speaking almost no English, and his integration into Canadian society began on that note.

Paul met Mary Nowak in September 1963 at the age of thirty-one. He walked into a Polish delicatessen one day to buy a zapiekanka, a Polish open-faced sandwich, to take to work for his supper, and a copy of the local Polish weekly newspaper to read while he ate. Mary's parents owned the deli. One thing led to another, and Paul and Mary married two years later, in 1965. They tried without success for nine years to have a child before adopting Ellie in 1974.

Now, all that was left of the little family they'd made was a tea pot and a book. Ludmila carefully wrapped and boxed both items, and Ellie locked them in her trunk for the drive home.

Paul was gone, disappeared into his grave for the rest of eternity, and now Mary as well.

This was Eleanor March at forty-five years of age.

Just short of the washroom door, they heard a huge crash coming from the front area of the building. They froze, and Junior's walkie-talkie crackled.

"Junior! Viens ici!"

Forgetting himself, perhaps because guarding people wasn't something he did very often, he propped Ellie against the wall and raced off to see what had happened.

Ellie fought back against the light-headedness, realizing she'd been given a chance to escape. She began to move, looking for a way out. She turned a corner and saw an Exit sign over a door at the end of the hallway.

There!

As she staggered toward it, a door opened and Squid stepped out.

"What the hell are you doing, bitch?"

"Get out of my way."

Lip curling, he strode up to her.

She tried to assume a martial arts defensive posture, but she was too clumsy. He swung at her. She tried to evade the blow, but it caught her on the ear. She went down. He grabbed her by the shirt and hauled her back to her feet. Slamming her against the wall, he pounded at her face and abdomen until he lost his grip and she slid to the floor.

After a few kicks to the ribs and groin, she was faintly aware of him dragging her along the hallway back to her room, where he chained her up and slammed the door on his way out.

CHAPTER 9

She had no idea how long she lay on the cot, slipping in and out of consciousness. Eventually her eyes stayed open and she stared at the ceiling. Her mouth was a little mashed up, so when Junior eventually arrived, he fed her soup through a straw, blaming himself the whole time.

She didn't feel like answering him, so she said nothing. Her left eye was swollen shut and her ribs hurt. She thought one or two of them might be cracked. When she was done, he patted her on the shoulder and left.

She fervently hoped that whatever he'd put in the soup would act as a painkiller as well as a sedative, because every square inch of her body was sore. Squid had definitely done a number on her, and she knew it would take a while before she felt better. The bastard had instantly risen to the top of her payback's-a-bitch list, and when the time came . . .

There was an aftertaste in her mouth. She thought about it for a moment before realizing it was from the soup. Not the acrid, bitter aftertaste of the drug, but the flavour of mushroom. It reminded her of the wild mushroom soup Mary used to make for Paul. She called it *zupa Gryzbowa* in Polish and made it with dried porcini mushrooms imported in a jar from Poland. It was traditionally served on Christmas Eve, but Mary also served it to Paul on his birthday as a special treat. It had garlic, which Junior's soup lacked, and allspice, among other mysterious ingredients.

Mary's *zupa* reminded her of Paul's birthday when she was seven. In Grade Two. She'd made him a birthday card at school. The rest of the class was making Thanksgiving decorations, but she made a card featuring a turkey with a very pink wattle and glasses like Paul's, with "Happy Birthday!" scrawled across the top. When she proudly presented it to him at the dinner table between his mushroom soup and his *kotlet schabowy*, his breaded pork cutlets, he studied it solemnly and then looked at her over his glasses.

"Do you think I look like a turkey, Eleanor?"

She bravely resisted crying, although she wanted to.

He set it down next to his glass of water and patted it lightly. "This is the most wonderful birthday card I've ever received. Thank you very much, my little dear."

The memory faded and she fell asleep thinking about Paul's kind, old-world eyes.

CHAPTER 10

Later in the afternoon, Kevin and Liam made a stop at the Victorian red brick house on Drummond Street East to pay a visit to Luke Ferguson, who'd returned to work. Before going upstairs, Kevin saw that Janie was taking a Diet Pepsi break in the welcoming room. He waved at the redhead and gave Janie a kiss.

"Staying out of trouble, cowboy?"

He smiled. "Trying to. This is Liam Woolfson."

Janie shifted her pop can and shook his hand. "Take care of this guy for me, will you?"

"Sure. Not a problem."

"Make sure he wears his hat. Where is it? Did he leave it in the car?"

Liam tried not to look like a deer in the headlights. "Um, I think so."

"Make sure he wears it."

Upstairs, they found Luke at his desk. Nick Rush stood at a filing cabinet, riffling through a drawer.

"Just the pair I was looking for," Kevin said, dropping into a chair. "Got a question for you."

"Yeah, well, I've got a question for you, too," Luke glared.

"Mine first. There's been a string of high-end car thefts in the area. Know anything about it?"

Luke said, "If you're asking me about my motorcycle club friends, then the answer's No. They're not into that scene."

Nick closed the file drawer, a folder in his hand. "Haven't come across anything lately, Kevin. Is that what you're working on right now?"

"Yeah. This is Detective Constable Woolfson, Nick."

Nick came over and shook hands before glancing at Luke.

"We've met," Luke grumbled. "What I want to know is when you're gonna start working on my friend's problem."

"Maybe soon, if you could point us to somebody who might be able to help us out with the cars. Maybe in exchange for the work I'm putting in on the outboard motor thing."

Nick turned away to hide a smile on his face.

"Horse trader, are you, Walker?" Luke grumbled.

"I can be."

"Shit. All right, let me think for a second."

Nick turned to Liam. "So, where are you from?"

"Thunder Bay."

"Really? I dated a girl once from Thunder Bay. Four inches taller than me."

Liam said, "She was so tall, no matter where she went she could always see her house."

"Don't get him started," Kevin said.

"She was so tall, when she tripped and fell she had time to call 911 before she hit the ground."

"That one sucks, Liam."

"Yeah, I know."

"Okay," Luke interrupted. "Against my better judgment. Let me call someone. If they're okay with it, they'll talk to you."

"When will this be, Luke?"

"Tonight."

CHAPTER 11

That evening, Kevin and Liam sat in the first-base bleachers at the town baseball field, watching a girls' little league softball game between a local squad of teenagers and a team of visitors from Stittsville.

The parking area behind the right-field fence was filled with vehicles, and the stands were crowded with parents, boyfriends, and bored townspeople looking for some free entertainment on a hot, muggy August evening.

Kevin smiled as a girl who reminded him of Caitlyn stroked a base hit to left field. "So, Liam."

"So, Kevin."

"What's the deal with all the bad jokes?"

Liam shrugged. "Long story."

"We're early," Kevin said. "We've got a few minutes."

A long sigh. "Sure, whatever." Another, shorter sigh.

"So, I'm from T-Bay, right?"

"Yeah, you've mentioned that."

"My parents ran a night club on the Port Arthur side called Arthur's Refuge. It was the best spot in the city for music and comedy acts." He smiled. "I grew up hanging around behind the bar, helping to stock the fridges and change the beer kegs. It was very cool. When I was twelve, Pearl Jam played the Fort William Gardens and came over to our place afterwards to jam with the house band. Unbelievable."

"Nice."

"After that we had Chilliwack, Prism, Trooper. You name it, they all came in."

"Wow."

"There were a lot of good stand-up comics who did the place, too, but they were mostly locals you would never have heard of. But I liked them the best."

"Is that why you always wanted to be a comedian?"

He laughed. "Hell, no. I already *was* a comic." He waggled his hand in the air. "Class clown, that was me. My grades sure sucked, but my material was great. I stole all my best one-liners from the club. That was how I kept from getting beaten up in school: entertaining the troops."

"So when did you—"

A man sat down next to Kevin. "You must be the cops. You two stick out like a pair of sore thumbs."

"My thumb's not the only thing that's sore," Liam said, waggling his bottom.

The man offered his hand. "The name's Cordwainer.

Evan Cordwainer. People call me Cord."

They shook hands all around. He was a squat little fellow in a white golf shirt, khaki shorts, over-the-calf black socks, and white Skechers. He tipped back his driver's cap and gave them a solemn look.

"I too was once a humble servant of the public, but retirement isn't treating me as kindly as I thought it might. Inflation's a nasty thing, you know."

He let go of Kevin but kept his hand out, palm up.

Kevin reached into his pocket and passed over five twenties in a tight little roll held with an elastic band. Cord removed the elastic, counted the money, and rolled it back up.

"It'll have to do," he said, making it disappear with a quick movement. "Beggars can't be choosers."

"You guys have the exact same hat," Liam said.

Cord frowned. "I think not. Mine is a genuine Irish wool driving cap. His looks like polyester. Am I right, sir?"

Kevin shrugged, not wanting to get into a hat war with the guy.

"What kind of public servant were you?" Liam asked.

"A good question. I worked for the Solicitor General, God bless him. Several solicitors general, in fact. And to save you the next question, I was a parole officer. A monitor of men, assisting in their reintegration into society, questioning their accountability; laying on the wood when necessary, praising and encouraging otherwise. What a load of bloody bull."

"Luke thought you might be able to—"

"Careful with names," Cord interrupted. "I've given you my real name because I'm not afraid of anyone, man nor beast, but others must remain anonymous. Is that understood?"

"Sure," Liam said.

"Very well. You want to talk about stolen cars."

"That's right," Kevin said. "We're looking for a cooling down spot somewhere around here where these cars are being kept before they're shipped out. Probably to Montreal for exportation overseas."

"Mmm. Yes." His chubby face took on a faraway look. "I had a customer name of Sylvester Foxworthy, went by the predictable name of Sly Fox. He was a mechanic working in a chop shop in Toronto that got raided by the TPS in one of their projects. After he served his time and was released, he came back here, to the Carleton Place area, to live with his dad.

"Quiet little fellow, didn't say a lot. Always filled out the forms on time and stayed in touch. He had a job in a muffler shop. I asked him one time if he thought about getting back into the business, and he was pretty adamant that it wasn't an option for him. Said the shop around here was a lot tougher than where he'd worked in Toronto. Too tough for his blood. And he had his father to think of."

Kevin waited. Liam took out a chunk of bubble gum, unwrapped it, and slipped it into his mouth.

"He let slip one day it was set up and run by a guy named Bruno. Mean sonofabitch. Didn't know his last name and had never seen him; it was just word of mouth."

"We'd like to talk to this Sly Fox," Kevin said.

"You'll have to hire a medium with a good crystal ball," he said. "He's dead. Lung cancer."

Liam leaned forward to stare past Kevin at Cord. "Bruno, eh? Hardly seems like it's worth a hundred bucks."

"You pays your money and you takes your chances, son." He held up a business card that had only a phone number on it. "Memorize it. If you need me again, I'm at your service."

CHAPTER 12

They left Ellie alone for the rest of the day and all that night. She lay on the cot, her thoughts tumbling around in every possible direction. She worried especially about Reggie, stuck inside the cottage. He'd been left alone for long stretches before, of course, but she'd always made sure to leave out extra food and water. This time there'd been no chance to do so. She'd thought she'd be going straight home after work.

The humidity in the air carried a number of distinctive odours from other parts of the building. She'd caught the scent of ozone, exhaust, grease, and gasoline. Her mind was like a poorly tuned radio right now, but she had enough sense to figure out that she was inside some kind of chop shop operation. Hence the black Thunderbird, her nightmare hearse—obviously just stolen—and the panicky response of Squid and his accomplice when she'd interrupted their escape.

A chop shop, yes, but the Thunderbird hadn't seemed to her a likely candidate for stripping and cubing. It was a genuine antique, not one of the design revivals Ford had issued between 2002 and 2005. So they must be dealing in stolen vehicles as well, part of the big upswing in car thefts feeding the greedy overseas black markets.

It reminded her that her ex-husband Gareth had treated himself to a 1972 blue Mustang a year or so before their divorce. He drove it all that summer and put it into storage in October. He left it there for a year and ended up selling it to a fellow Conservative Party of Canada worker who was also going through a mid-life crisis.

She'd never driven it. She'd had no real desire to. She wasn't interested in cars. She'd been trained to drive a stick-shift as part of her driving course at police college, but she didn't attach any particular mystique to it. In general, she had a decent knowledge of vintage cars which she'd built up through experience on the job, but they didn't stir any particular emotion in her as they did with some people.

Someone like Leif Brand, for example. Now, there was a guy she hadn't thought about for a long time. A good man, and a good friend. Again, 2002. Her first stint as a detective constable, and Brand assigned to her as a babysitter. He loved muscle cars without ever having owned one. Couldn't afford it.

Thinking about Brand brought back memories of her first major crime investigation, which took place in the autumn of that year. A disappearance; an unexplained death; a messy, upsetting post-mortem; and the opportunity for her to show that she either had what it would take to be a detective, or should go back to Traffic and just stay there.

SEPTEMBER 2002

CHAPTER 13

Ontario Provincial Police Detective Constable Ellie March stood in the doorway of Leif Brand's cubicle in the South Wellington Operations Centre in Rockwood, Guelph/Eramosa Township, and cleared her throat.

She held a Tim Hortons cardboard tray in her hand with two extra large coffees and all the fixings piled into the other holes. There was nowhere to put it down, because every square centimeter of Brand's desktop space was taken up with clutter.

"Where the hell you been?" he demanded, swiveling around. "You're late."

She held up the tray. "Want it or not?"

He reached out and took one of the coffees, disdaining the creamers and packets of sugar. "Stopping for coffee's no excuse, Eleanor. You need to build the extra time into your schedule."

"Come on, Leif, I'm five minutes early."

"You need to be fifteen early. How many times do I have to say it?"

"My commute's over an hour. A lot of opportunities for time contraction beyond my control."

He laughed. "Time contraction? Jesus."

This was Eleanor March at twenty-nine years of age.

She'd just finished her specialized training a month ago, after having been appointed as a detective constable assigned to the Wellington County Crime Unit. She was partnered up with Brand, a difficult man to get used to.

She was a week in as his protégé when he invited her out for a drink and a motel room after their shift. She'd laughed in his face and said if he mentioned it again she'd invite his wife out for a drink and a long talk after her shift.

She'd caught a brief smirk before he walked away. He played it straight thereafter, and Ellie soon understood that he'd been testing her, wanting to see which way she'd jump. This belief was confirmed when she learned from others that he didn't drink and was a devoted family man. In the future, Kevin Walker would remind her of him in this regard.

Brand had just taken his first sip of coffee when his desk phone rang. It was the crime unit sergeant, assigning them a call out.

The date was Saturday, June 8, 2002, and the time was 12:07 PM. They drove five kilometers from Rockwood to the home of Justin Paige on 5th Line Road, Brucedale, a hamlet about thirteen kilometers north of Guelph.

Paige was crowding forty, a curly-haired little guy with black frame glasses, a skinny neck, and an expensive casual wardrobe. His house wasn't anything special, just a twenty-year-old, ranch-style bungalow with burgundy and cream siding, but his property extended back from the road in a six-acre rectangle, and the grounds were nicely tended with gardens, lilac bushes, and a flowering crab tree. His vehicle was an expensive black pickup truck with not a lot of road dust on it, suggesting he took it through the car wash in Guelph on a regular basis.

Brand led the way in, and they sat in Paige's living room to get the story.

"I was out in the back garden all morning," he said. "I have a lot of tomatoes, and I was filling a basket to do some canning. Cindy was sleeping in. I came in for lunch and she was gone."

"Any signs of a disturbance?" Brand asked. "Anything missing, like clothing or a knapsack, that might indicate she'd taken off somewhere?"

"No, no. That's just it. She hadn't made her bed, but she'd gotten dressed. She ate breakfast. A bowl of cereal. It's still on the counter."

"A normal Saturday morning for her?" Ellie asked.

"Yes, completely normal."

"So what did you do?"

"I started calling her friends, but none of them had seen her. I called my ex-wife, but it went to voicemail. I got in the car and drove around Brucedale, looked in at the restaurant: nothing. By that time I was getting upset, so I called the police."

"Tell us about your ex-wife," Brand said. "Did your daughter get along with her?"

Paige grimaced. "No. Not at all. Dawn is my—was my—second wife. Cindy's mother was Theresa. She died when Cindy was six."

"How long ago did you divorce?"

"A year ago. Cindy was twelve."

"So, they didn't get along?"

"They hated each other. Oh, Dawn tried at first, but Cindy wouldn't give her an inch. There was no way she was going to replace her mother, and that's all there was to it."

"Do you have a recent photograph we could take with us?" Ellie asked.

"Sure." He went over to the fireplace and removed a five-by-seven picture from a porcelain frame. "It's a selfie of the two of us in the garden last summer," he said, handing it to her. "Cindy doesn't like to have her picture taken, so it was a miracle I was able to get her to stand still long enough to take this one."

Paige looked happy in the photo while his daughter, a slender, pretty blonde, radiated discomfort. Ellie tucked it into the pages of her notebook.

"Don't worry, Mr. Paige," she said. "We'll find her for you."

CHAPTER 14

Leif Brand was genuinely angry with her. He slammed the car door and strode through the parking lot, leaving Ellie behind. She followed him inside to his cubicle, where she leaned on the doorframe and folded her arms.

"What? What is it?"

He whirled around, his chair squeaking loudly. "Never say that again."

"Say what?"

"Never write cheques that your ass can't cash, Eleanor. Never, ever, say 'Don't worry. We'll find her.' It's unprofessional, it's unfair to the family member, and it's just damned stupid."

She was taken aback by the vehemence with which he said it. "I'm sorry."

"If something's happened to that kid, how in the hell are you going to go back to that man and tell him your word's no good, that you failed him, that—"

"I hate to interrupt," Sergeant Morrow said, appearing behind Ellie, "but you're going to have to go right back out. A body part has been found on a hiking trail just above the Guelph Lake Conservation Area. Take Eleanor down there, Leif, and see if she's going to have to deliver that bad news you're talking about."

"Shit. Damn. Hell." Brand stood up. "Wait for me in the car," he said to Ellie. "I gotta take a piss."

The car, of course, was locked, so she leaned against the passenger door, watching a constable get out of his cruiser and cross the parking lot. As he passed, he winked at her.

She hadn't been here long enough to become acquainted with all the uniformed personnel, and this guy was a stranger to her. Young; beefy; slick.

There were only two other sworn officers on staff at this command centre in 2002 who were female. One handled media relations and the other worked in Traffic. The men viewed them either with annoyance or amusement, and it was always an uphill battle to achieve any kind of respect as an equal. Ellie had experienced it for five years as a provincial constable driving a cruiser in Grey County, and had learned to block it out and concentrate on her job performance.

At the moment, though, having screwed up and taken a verbal tearing-down for it, she wasn't mentally prepared to ignore the guy and his wink. It seemed to put her in her place, reinforce Leif's frustrations and anger with her.

And there was no point in her being defensive about it because, damn it, he was right. She'd made a mistake.

In the car, Brand started the engine and looked over at her.

"I'm sorry," she said. "Lesson learned."

He nodded and backed out of the parking space.

By the time they arrived at the hiking trail, the coroner, an older man named Dr. George Baldeski, was already there. The incident commander, Sergeant Bradley, recited the basics. Hikers walking the trail had come across a coyote or bush wolf with something in its mouth. Startled, the animal dropped the object and ran away. When they got close, they could see it was a human hand. They called 911.

A search team had been organized to look for more body parts. Three teams of ERT were on the job, and a paramedic had gone out with each to bag any parts that were found.

The coroner showed them the hand, now in an evidence bag. It was white, slender, and narrow. A right hand. There were two rings: a gold-plated one with a tiny four-leaf clover, on the middle finger; and an adjustable sterling silver ring on the thumb featuring a simple knot.

A girl's hand. A teenaged girl's hand.

"What we have here," Baldeski told them, "is a case

of animal scavenging, which is a natural process in what we call 'taphonomy.' This term," he continued, looking at Ellie, "refers to anything that happens to a body after death."

He held up the bag and pointed to the wrist stump. "See the tooth marks and tearing wounds? Likely a pack that came across the corpse during the night and fought amongst themselves for the best parts. I'd say the fellow who ended up with this was low on the totem pole, since there's not a lot of meat on the bones of your average hand."

Ellie nodded, hiding her revulsion.

"We see that she fell from that cliff up there," he pointed, "down onto the rocks, there," he pointed again. "Her limbs, head, and feet have been carted away, but the torso's still here, although badly ravaged. I know it's a her because of the pelvis, which animals are least likely to disturb. You can look at it if you like, but most of the meat's already been ripped away."

"We're good," Brand said.

The witnesses who found the hand were waiting for them at the car park where the trail began. They were leaning against the fender of their car, under the watchful eye of a uniformed constable.

"I'm Detective Constable Brand, OPP. This is Detective Constable March. Your names?"

"Steve Brownlow," answered the male.

"Victoria Maitland."

"Steve; Victoria. All right if I call you that?"

"Yeah."

The female nodded.

"So, you two are from Guelph?"

"Yeah," Brownlow said. "We're both grad students at the U. I'm doing a Master's in Philosophy, and Vic is in Music."

"Up here for a little fresh air and exercise, eh?"

"Yeah."

They were both kitted up as typical hipsters on a country outing, with the berets, hiking boots, and khaki shorts with patch pockets and belt loops hanging with stuff. The expressions on their faces, though, left no doubt in Ellie's mind that the fun was done.

"So tell me what happened."

They glanced at each other before Brownlow spoke. "We were following the trail where it bends around the cliff formation. You can get up there, too, if you take an offshoot, but we never bother. We had just rounded the curve when we saw this wolf or coyote or whatever it was standing there about six meters away from us. We stopped. It had something in its mouth, but it dropped it and ran away. We waited for a moment but it didn't come back, so we walked up to see what it had dropped. I—"

The female, Maitland, pressed the back of her hand to her mouth and closed her eyes.

"We, uh, threw up. I know you're not supposed to contaminate a crime scene, but we couldn't help it."

"Don't worry about it. Did either of you touch the hand?"

"Are you kidding?" Maitland managed, gulping.

"No," Brownlow added.

Brand looked at Ellie.

"If there's anything else you think we should know," she said, giving each of them a business card, "please call."

"All right."

"The officer here will get your addresses and phone numbers," she added, "and we'll ask you to come to Rockwood later for official statements."

"Okay."

They went back to the rock pile, where Dr. Baldeski had set up a folding table to process the body parts as they came in.

"Ah, there you are. Come look at this, detectives."

Sitting on the table next to a body bag containing the torso was a foot in an evidence bag, and another part that Ellie could not see until she reached the table.

The girl's head.

Straight blond hair, with a barrette still in place. One cheek torn completely off, the other half-eaten. Eyes gone. Lips gone. Teeth stained with blood. The right temple crushed in, likely from where it had struck a rock at the bottom of the cliff.

Ellie's stomach heaved. She fought to control it. The nausea passed. She was all right. She knew, right then and there, that she'd never have trouble with her stomach at a crime scene again. She could handle it.

She was aware that Brand was watching her.

She bent over for a closer look.

"The teeth will likely allow us to make an identification through dental records," Baldeski said. "There's been some work done, so it's just a matter of finding the correct dentist."

"Yes," she said, although she already knew in her heart who it was. Cindy Paige.

This was Eleanor March at twenty-nine years of age.

PRESENT DAY

CHAPTER 15

On Wednesday morning, Kevin spooned down his Coco Puffs breakfast while staring at the empty seat at the table that used to be occupied by his step-daughter, Caitlyn. He missed her terribly.

Caitlyn had moved out. In his mind, she was still a child requiring his protection and guidance, but the truth of the matter was that she was a young woman who had flown the nest and was now in charge of her own life.

She'd graduated high school at the end of June and had been awarded a Chancellor's Scholarship at Carleton University in Ottawa. It was worth $30 thousand that would be renewable each year of her undergraduate studies because her grade average had been over 90 per cent and her extra-curricular activities, which had included year book editor and contributor, volunteer in the school library, and Justice Action Committee participant, had more than met Carleton's requirements.

Kevin and Janie were very proud of her, especially because the scholarship amount was the highest available from the university. They were also relieved because they would never have been able to afford her tuition and expenses.

She'd moved into a room in the home of her mentor, Dr. Sara Narayan, a young associate professor of psychology at Carleton. Classes weren't due to begin until September 9, but Dr. Narayan had suggested that Caitlyn spend the month of August with her, preparing for university life and getting in some advanced reading for the courses she'd selected.

Kevin recalled with warmth the excitement in her eyes when they'd helped her move in. Books; clothing; mementos; her laptop; and framed photos of everyone, including her cat, Boo Boo. Dr. Narayan ("please, call me Sara") assured them that Cait was in good hands and would be just fine.

Janie cried all the way home.

Kevin's jaw ached from holding it in. He kept his eyes on the highway, barely seeing the pavement, driving on auto-pilot, his brain locked down.

Charlotte let out a shriek, startling him out of his daydream. Kevin and Janie had won the war to get their feisty little eighteen-month-old to stay at the table until they said she could leave, but she didn't like it one bit.

Janie said, "Are you done?"

Charlotte let out another shriek, pointing at her bowl. There was still some yogurt and granola left, but she'd eaten all her raspberries.

"Do you want another raspberry?" Janie took one from her bowl and put it in Charlotte's. She pounced on it right away and gobbled it up.

Kevin took out his phone and called Ellie. Straight to voicemail. Definitely not like her. Now he was worried. He considered the possibility she'd just gone offline for a while to take care of something in her personal life. Then he reconsidered; Ellie didn't seem to have a personal life.

Perhaps it was time to stop giving her the benefit of the doubt and track her down.

CHAPTER 16

Kevin was a hunt-and-peck typist, so there were days when it was a challenge to run systems checks, particularly when he was distracted by something. For example, not knowing Ellie's whereabouts and being increasingly worried about it.

He botched a query and had to re-enter the search term, grumbling under his breath.

Bruno.

He'd run it through several systems, with a null result each time. Same thing once again.

He tipped back his head and closed his eyes, straining for inspiration. Liam and Alaric were huddled in the comm room, scanning maps for possible warehouses or sheds where a cooling spot might be located.

"What's up, Kevin?"

He startled, his eyes snapping open. "Damn,

Heather!"

"Wakey-wakey. I'm looking for a ride. Who wants to go talk to a guy who just had his black Thunderbird stolen?"

"Where?"

"Here in town. He's waiting on us."

Kevin logged off and reached for his jacket, then changed his mind. It was too damned hot and muggy to stand on ceremony today. Leaving his hat on its hook as well, he shoved his notebook into his jeans, dropped a pen into his shirt pocket, and nodded.

"Let's go."

In the car, Heather said, "I've been meaning to ask how the baby's doing."

"She's doing fine, thanks. Barb thinks she might be ready to start potty training soon. It's a little early; she's only eighteen months and it usually starts around when they turn two, but we'll see."

Barb, Janie's mother, lived in the other half of the duplex they'd bought on Cockburn Street. She looked after Charlotte during the day while they were at work.

"How'd she get the name, by the way?"

Kevin laughed. "Oh, that was Caitlyn. Janie gave her naming privileges, so she chose Charlotte because *Charlotte's Web* was her favourite story when she was a kid. Leave it to her to name our last child after a book."

"Last, eh?"

"Yeah."

Alex Powell lived in a beautiful two-storey brick home on Sheppard Avenue. They walked up the driveway past a late-model Range Rover parked in front of the garage.

"Unlocked," Heather remarked.

Powell answered the door a few seconds after Kevin rang the bell. He was tall and skinny, with white marcelled hair and a white pencil moustache. Heather leaned over and whispered, "Cesar Romero."

Kevin knew who that was but he frowned just the same.

Powell took them into his den and poured coffee all around. They sat and sipped.

"I'm a chemical process engineer," Powell said from behind his desk, tilting back in his swivel chair. "Retired, of course. Spent nearly forty years in the industry, the last decade with Trygram and Markson here in town."

"Decent pay?" Heather asked. This was her show. Kevin was the self-appointed note taker for this one.

"You could say that." He smiled, not offended by the question.

She looked around the room, which was filled with golf trophies and memorabilia and assorted collectibles. "You're big into golf, are you?"

"Yes, I am. Walking eighteen holes once a week is great exercise at my age. Do you play?"

"Can't stand golf."

"Well, it's an enjoyable summer hobby, anyway."

"What do you do in the winter, Mr. Powell?"

"Call me Alex. Well, let's see, this past winter I spent most of my time on my other hobby."

"Which is?"

"I collect comic books."

Kevin thought Heather was going to burst a blood vessel.

"No kidding! So do I!"

"That's nice. How many in your collection?"

"Something over six thousand," Heather replied.

"That's very good."

"What about you?"

Powell smiled indulgently. "I have eleven thousand, four hundred, and ninety ... something. You can see why it took me the winter to catalogue them."

"Do you ever trade?"

"Occasionally," he replied, cautiously. "Do you have something in mind?"

Heather's eyes narrowed. "What are you looking for?"

Powell thought for a moment. Kevin figured he was trying to decide if Heather was actually a serious collector or just an overgrown kid with Archie comics and a few boxes of junk put out by Image, Topps, and Malibu that were worth next to nothing.

"I'm a big Green Lantern guy," he finally said. "The Silver Age version, and of course his first appearance was in *Showcase* 22.

"Drawn by Gil Kane," Heather said.

His eyes widened a little. "That's correct."

"Worth about thirty-two grand," she said.

"It can be, in Mint condition. Unfortunately I only have a placeholder in my collection right now. A 2.0, worth about two thousand.

"What about a grade of 4.0?" she asked casually.

"About forty-five hundred. Why?"

"I have one slabbed and graded Very Good at 4.2."

"Nice. Are you saying you'd be willing to part with it?"

"I might be." She thought for a moment. "I'm big into *Magnus Robot Fighter*. But my copy of number one is a rat chew that would be lucky to grade at around 1.5."

He laughed. "That's definitely what you would call a placeholder." He eyed her for a moment. "As it happens, I have three copies of that book. I'd be willing to offer you the one graded 9.2 in exchange for your *Showcase*."

"What's it worth?"

"About thirty six hundred," he replied, after a brief search of his memory. "Around a thousand dollars difference. What else would you like to sweeten the pot?"

Kevin watched her suppress a smile as she looked away, thinking about it. He couldn't help but enjoy the show.

"Got any *Hot Stuff*?" she finally asked.

"The Harvey books, I presume."

"Of course. I'm looking for Number 1."

Alex sat up and brought his laptop out of sleep mode. "Okay, we're talking about issue one, October 1957. Correct?"

"Yes, indeed."

Click, clack, clack.

"I have a couple," he said, studying his monitor. "The one graded 5.0 is worth about twelve hundred. I think we could call it even."

Heather rested her chin in her palm, as though thinking

about it. "So, I'll trade you my *Showcase* 22, and you'll give me *Magnus* 1 and *Hot Stuff* 1. Is that right?"

Powell stroked his moustache. "I think that would be a fair trade. Don't you?"

Kevin watched them shake hands on it and exchange business cards.

"I'll call you tomorrow, shall I?"

"Sure," Heather said. "We'll set it up then."

Kevin could hear the excitement in her voice. To him it sounded like Monopoly money being exchanged.

He cleared his throat. "How long have you owned the Thunderbird, Alex?"

"What? Oh, yes." Powell chuckled with embarrassment. "My apologies. It's not often you meet a fellow collector by chance like this. We'll have to see what other business we can do," he added, addressing Heather.

She nodded. "Did you have the car for quite a while?"

"About four years. It was a retirement present from my wife."

"Is she here right now?"

"Actually no, she's out in Calgary visiting our son. She's trying to persuade him to move back to Ontario before those idiots try to separate from Canada and become the fifty-first state. Brainless morons. I keep saying they're welcome to leave whenever they want. They just can't take our province with them."

"I notice you have a Range Rover in the driveway," Kevin said.

Powell nodded.

"It looks like it might be unlocked."

"Yes, I guess so. I never pay attention."

"Was the Thunderbird unlocked?"

"I guess it probably was."

Kevin marvelled, not for the first time in his career, at how cavalier wealthy people could be when it came to important but basic routines to safeguard their possessions.

"With all due respect sir, that was probably a contributing factor to the theft."

Powell nodded again, ruefully.

Heather leaned forward. "Did you notice anyone suspicious on your street over the past few days?"

"No, not really. Again, I don't pay a lot of attention to that sort of thing."

"When did you realize it had been stolen?"

"Well, I heard it start up and back out of the driveway. By the time I got to the front door it was already gone. So I went and called you folks right away."

Kevin had pretty much decided that they weren't going to get anything useful from the interview when Alex said, "My friend Pete called after I called you. He said he thought he saw the car up at the McDonald's, in some kind of fender bender. A couple of guys were standing around, and a woman. I hope it wasn't mine. I can't stand the thought of it being involved in an accident."

After they left, with Pete's name and number recorded in Kevin's notebook, they canvassed the street for an hour, knocking on doors and asking questions, but no one had noticed anyone suspicious on the street either in the past few days or at the time of the theft.

It seemed that eyewitnesses were as scarce as Green Lantern debut comic books on this street.

CHAPTER 17

No one brought her breakfast, but late in the morning Junior came into her room with a tray. She sucked soup through a straw, mindful of the small cuts on her lips, and ate a dinner roll, which he tore into strips and fed her a bit at a time.

The woman came in and took her to the washroom. When she came back, Junior turned his attention to the cuts on her forehead, the bridge of her nose, and her chin, cleaning them with rubbing alcohol, smearing them with antibiotic paste, and covering them with band-aids. They weren't quite serious enough to have required stitches, and had clotted over so that the bleeding had stopped. At least the swelling around her eye had gone down enough that she could see through it again.

She knew without having to be told that her nose had been broken. A brief glance in the washroom mirror had revealed to her a pair of black eyes and a nasty red bump between them. Plus, it hurt like hell.

She also had a number of bruises that were sore, but he only looked these over and sighed.

"I'm very sorry this happened."

"So am I." She looked at a bulge in the sleeve of his T-shirt where he'd folded in a pack of cigarettes. "Light one for me, will you?"

He took them out, lit one, and pushed it between her lips.

"Thanks."

"You're welcome. You remind me of my mama when she fell down the stairs one time. I spent a week looking after her. Cuts and bruises. Broke a finger and cracked her ribs. Are yours sore?"

"Yes. You had a mother, did you?"

He smiled, ignoring her sarcasm. "Still do. The best woman God ever put on this earth. She's a lot older than you are, of course, but still, this reminds me of her that time."

"Tell me about her," Ellie said, not particularly caring but wanting him to talk in case he said something of interest.

"Her name's Amoy. She's retired now, of course, and lives in a home. She's Creole, born in Jamaica. She came to Canada with her family. Very, very smart lady."

Ellie exhaled slowly, the cigarette helping her maintain

focus on what he was saying.

"She worked as an interpreter at Hôpital Marie-Clarac. They always need people who can speak the language. Jamaican Creole, I mean. I suppose it doesn't hurt to say this was in Montréal-Nord."

Ellie waved the cigarette as though she didn't particularly care one way or another what he revealed to her.

"She rode the bus every day to work. It was the only job she could find at the time. She loved what she did, but we lived in Côte-des-Neiges, so it was nearly an hour there and an hour home at the end of the day. She read books to pass the time. She liked poetry. Una Marson, Louise Bennett, Velma Pollard. I remember these names because she had a little shelf in the hallway just inside the front door where she kept her favourite books."

"Jamaicans?"

"Yes."

"What about your father?"

"He drove a taxi. His name was Gilles. Which is my name, too. That's why mama always calls me Junior."

"That's nice."

"He was white. They met one winter day when the bus wasn't running and she had to take a taxi to work. That was all it took." Junior laughed softly. "He wasn't nearly as smart as mama, but he was smart enough to know a good thing when he saw it."

Ellie held out the stub of her cigarette. Junior gave her the bowl that had contained her soup. She dropped in the butt and gave it back.

"She had to put up with a lot of racism," Junior said. "Her French was good, and she had to listen to a lot of crap from white Francophones. Sometimes I heard her talking to papa about it. It upset her. It made me mad. I—"

One of the other men stood in the doorway. "Bruno's here."

Junior hastily got to his feet.

"He wants to talk to her," the man said.

Ellie shrugged. "Fine by me."

CHAPTER 18

Bruno rolled into the room in a motorized wheelchair. Junior waited at the door in case he was ordered to do something.

"Mrs. March," Bruno said, "I regret that you've received such horrible treatment while in our hands."

"So do I," she replied once again, starting to sound like a broken record.

"You're a housekeeper, they tell me."

"Yes." She fought against the lightheadedness that she knew was a result of the sedative. "You don't need to keep me here, though. If you let me go, I won't say anything to anyone."

Bruno shook his head sadly. "It's not that simple." He massaged his face with a rough hand. It was a face gone flabby with the arrival of middle age and too much alcohol, which she could smell in his perspiration. Dark complected, dark brown eyes, black hair and thick black eyebrows.

He was shirtless, because of heat and humidity. He spoke with an accent Ellie struggled to place and his sentences were formally structured, as though English was not his first language.

"Why is it not so simple, Mr. Bruno? I'll give you my word."

"Ribeiro. Bruno Ribeiro. See? We treat you with a certain familiarity in order to lower your level of stress, but of course this must have long-term consequences."

"You mean at some point you're going to kill me."

"It is a possibility." He studied her face. "This does not seem to frighten you."

"I'm not afraid of death. Why should I be? I'll be asleep, so I won't know what's happening to me. I just won't ever wake up again, that's all."

"An admirable philosophy, Mrs. March." He rubbed his scruffy chin. "Are you a local?"

"I live down near Brockville."

"What were you doing in Perth, then?"

"Seeing a client."

"Junior tells me you're a housekeeper."

"Yeah."

"And your husband? You're widowed?"

"Mmm. He was a traveling salesman."

"I see. Selling what, exactly?"

She hesitated before thinking of Grant Burnham, a man whose murder they'd investigated a couple of years ago. "For a while, it was sporting goods. Then he switched to furniture."

"And how did he die?"

"At a furniture outlet. Like The Brick; I can't remember the name right now. A truck ran over him at the back of the store. It was filled with"—she was going to say mixed nuts, thinking of the Steve Martin movie she watched every Christmas, but decided it wasn't a good time to be a smartass—"mattresses."

"Unfortunate. My condolences." He stared at her, trying to decide if she were lying or telling the truth.

"I've gotten used to being alone."

"No children?"

She shook her head. "Couldn't have any."

He turned his wheelchair around and headed for the door. "Do not try again to escape. If you do, I'll shoot you myself. Is that understood?"

"Understood."

She slept most of the afternoon away. For supper they brought her a Whopper burger and a large Coke. She wolfed down the burger, noticing as she chewed that they hadn't completely crushed the tablet of whatever it was they were using to sedate her. She was too damned hungry to stop chewing long enough to fish the pieces out of her mouth.

After a bathroom trip, she was left alone for the rest of the night. She lay on the cot with her eyes closed, but she couldn't fall asleep. It was incredibly hot in the room. Her clothing was soaked with sweat. Her mind was restless, passing in and out of memories, random thoughts, and images of Reggie barking at her to get up in the morning to let him out. She wondered if Kevin had noticed she was missing. If he had, she knew damned well he'd be doing something about it.

She saw herself sitting at the end of a long row of desks in a classroom at the police college. She'd passed the candidate selection process without a problem. Her high school transcript was excellent; her vision tested well above minimum standards; her fitness logs, thanks to her participation in athletics at high school, showed that her running and strength training exceeded requirements; and her medical exam was spotless. She'd been assigned to the twelve-week training program, and was steadily making her way through it.

This was Eleanor March at nineteen years of age.

The classrooms were filled with men, most of them young, aggressive types with buzz cuts and biceps stretching the cuffs of their short-sleeved uniform shirts. There were two other females in her class, somewhere behind her in other rows, and one Black male.

Although she'd never handled a firearm before in her life, she breezed through the courses and almost immediately established herself as the best marksman in her class.

The instructor had shrugged and said, "Looks like you're a natural, March."

There she was, sitting at the end of a long row of desks, notebook and hat in front of her, listening to a lecture on legislative authorities. The instructor was a grey-haired son of a bitch named Thompson who hated all cadets and especially hated females.

"March!"

"Yes, sir!"

"Name the five areas of responsibilities for a police constable as specified in the *Police Services Act*."

"Yes, sir. Preserving the peace; preventing crime and assisting others in the prevention of crime; executing warrants; assisting crime victims; and catching offenders and charging their sorry asses, sir."

"You have a smart mouth, March. Also a good memory. Do you have the rest of the *Act* memorized too?"

"Yes, sir."

"Get your nose out of his ass, bitch," muttered the guy sitting behind her.

Eleanor March, nineteen and brimming with self-confidence, repressed a smirk. Thompson was staring at her, just waiting for it, but she wouldn't give him the satisfaction.

She'd graduate from this dump at the top of her class if it half-killed her to do so.

Tossing and turning on the cot, she finally dozed for a while. Consciousness, when it returned, was a little confused. She found herself back with Leif Brand, driving to Guelph.

CHAPTER 19

Brand glanced over at her, his big hands loose on the steering wheel. "You okay?"

"Sure." Ellie kept her tone nonchalant, as though nothing unusual had happened in the last hour.

"I saw you suck it up back there."

She nodded, watching the scenery pass by. The girl's head had thrown her, but she'd compartmentalized it in a corner of her mind she hoped she'd never have to access again.

"You also handled Paige well."

"Thanks."

She'd called the girl's father from the scene to ask if they could send someone for a sample of Cindy's fingerprints. He told her there was a child's identification kit in the refrigerator, the sort of thing that community services police officers put together for parents visiting their booth at local fairs and Canada Day shows. It hadn't occurred to either of them to ask about prints before, as they were working at that point on the assumption that the girl was still alive, but it was something Ellie filed away for future reference.

A constable picked up the ID kit and brought it back. Dr. Baldeski matched the prints in the kit with prints from the severed hand.

It was Cindy Paige.

It was then Ellie's responsibility to notify Justin Paige of his daughter's death. Brand drove her to the house on 5th Line Road, where they followed Paige into the living room. Ellie gave him the bad news.

She watched him weep for several moments before murmuring, "I'm very, very sorry."

"I knew something was terribly wrong," he said between his fingers. "What happened?"

"She was found on the hiking trail south of here, near Guelph Lake. Do you have any idea how she might have gotten there?"

He shook his head. "Makes no sense. No sense at all. How does she go from having breakfast here to being found dead in the wilderness?"

"Is this a place she'd gone to before?"

He nodded.

Ellie glanced at Brand, who made a small motion with his head toward the door. He stood up, taking out his cellphone, and left the room.

"Is there someone who could drop by and be with you

for a while?" Ellie asked. "A family member? A neighbour or a friend?"

He said nothing.

"Is there a pastor or minister we could call for you?"

"No. Thanks."

Brand came back in. "Ten minutes."

Ellie nodded. "Detective Constable Brand called our office, and they're sending some support people from the Fergus crisis services team to talk to you after we leave."

"I don't need anyone. I'm fine."

"That's good, I'm glad to hear it, but they're very nice people. You can talk to them about anything at all and they won't mind."

Paige wept silently, hiding his face in his hands.

Ellie stopped talking, sensing that silence was the best course of action for the moment.

After what seemed like an eternity, the doorbell rang. Brand got up to answer it. There were two of them, a man and a woman, both middle-aged with kindly faces and soft voices. They introduced themselves to Paige, allowing Ellie and Brand to express their condolences once again and leave.

Brand drove in silence for a few kilometers. "The other thing I noticed," he finally said, referring to her behaviour at the scene of Cindy's death, "was the look you gave Simms and Remsberg."

Ellie made a noise in her throat. "They're not as funny as they think they are."

"Not a fan of gallows humour?"

Ellie's lip curled. Simms and Remsberg were forensic identification constables who were working the scene and lending a hand to Dr. Baldeski during his field assessment.

"No, I'm not a fan. For one thing, they were joking about a young girl who died a horrible death. For another, they had to be spoken to before they'd shut up. It was inappropriate."

"So, what did you think of Duncan?"

Detective Inspector Carol Duncan had attended the scene as the major case manager assigned from the Criminal Investigation Branch at GHQ in Orillia. She was one of the first such managers, the MCM process having only recently been implemented after the conviction of serial killer Paul Bernardo in 1995 and the subsequent report issued by Justice Archie Campbell on the shortcomings exposed by the case in information sharing within multi-jurisdictional investigations.

Duncan was the only woman currently assigned to the CIB. She'd listened to Brand's situation report, nodding to Ellie while eyeing her speculatively, and then walked off with Sergeant Bradley to confer with Dr. Baldeski.

Ellie watched her like a hawk. While many women in policing wore their hair short or pulled back and pinned in a tight bun—Ellie herself preferring the former—Carol Duncan's hair fell across her shoulders in unruly auburn waves. Her eyebrows were tawny, and her complexion was as smooth as porcelain.

Her voice was an even, calm contralto.

The words she spoke to Simms and Remsberg were direct and succinct. The two doofuses fell silent immediately and their chins dropped as they focused on their work, faces red with embarrassment.

Ellie had read that as of that point in time, 2002, only 3.9 per cent of commissioned police officers in *Canada* were women, while the total of all Canadian officers, including constables, non-commissioned officers, and commissioned officers, was just over 15 per cent female. Within the OPP, by comparison, they'd reached 17 per cent. Slightly better, but still too low, as far as Ellie was concerned.

Carol Duncan, recruited from the RCMP into CIB to change things up, was a harbinger of things to come, she hoped.

While she would always think of Leif Brand as her mentor, the one who taught her how to be a detective, Eleanor March knew right then and there, at the age of twenty-nine, that she'd found her role model, the person whose career would inspire her own. Some day, she'd be commissioned as an inspector in the force, just like Carol Duncan. Some day, she'd lead teams of investigators as they solved horrible and traumatic crimes.

Some day, she'd be just like Detective Inspector Carol Duncan.

CHAPTER 20

When Dawn Paige opened the door to them at her modest two-bedroom home in the north end of Guelph, she wore a white terry bathrobe, white slip-on sneakers, and tinted glasses with white frames.

"Come on in, I'm just doing a laundry. I got some time."

She led them into a sitting room with a couch, two recliners, and a television set. "I can hear the washer from in here," she said, sitting down, "so I know when to go throw stuff in the dryer."

"We appreciate your giving us the time," Ellie said. "We're very sorry to inform you that your step-daughter, Cindy Paige, has lost her life."

"Oh, no. What a terrible shame. What happened?"

"She was found deceased at a hiking trail south of her home, near Guelph Lake."

"That's awful." She looked away. In her mid-thirties, Dawn carried about fifteen pounds more than was ideal for her short frame, although some of it had been generously allotted to her bust line. Her hair was dyed blond and showed brown roots. Her blue eyes were hooded and expressionless.

Moisture brimmed along her lower lids, but Ellie immediately wondered if they were crocodile tears. Dawn didn't seem to be as upset as one might think she would be by such devastating news.

"Did you know she was missing?"

Dawn nodded. "Justin called to see if she was here. Fat chance."

"You and she didn't get along?"

"Nope. Me and her never saw eye to eye, not from Day One. I wasn't her mother, and that's all there was to it."

"What about you? How did you feel about her?"

"Me? Oh, lord knows I tried. I really did. I bought her stuff, made her special things to eat she turned her nose up at, did her laundry, the works. None of it mattered. She was just a spoiled little princess. A daddy's girl, and that's a club nobody else can join, believe me."

"When was the last time you saw her?"

"About two weeks ago. I went around to pick up some stuff I'd left in the basement. A couple of boxes. You would have thought I was robbing a bank or something. She yapped at me the whole time I was there. Little bitch."

"That's the last time you saw her."

"Yeah, that's what I just said."

"What about talk to her on the phone?"

"Her and I don't talk on the phone. That'd be the day."

"Where were you on Saturday?"

"Shopping."

"Where'd you go?"

"Stone Road. The mall."

"Would you happen to have any receipts from your purchases that would show us where you were?"

"I don't keep receipts. I throw them out with the bags. What is this, anyway? Why are you asking me where I was and all this stuff?"

"Just routine. Would there be anyone at the mall who would remember you being there? Any clerks you're familiar with or friends you might have bumped into who could vouch for you?"

"I don't know anyone who works there, and I don't have a lot of friends. But I did have an argument with a bossy little clerk at Zellers who tried to tell me what line to stand in. Little bitch. She might remember me. I gave *her* the time of day."

"Who else lives here in the house with you?"

"Just my boyfriend."

"What's his name?"

"Bill. Bill Orton. The lease's in his name. I just help with the rent."

"What does he do for a living?"

"He works at the chip factory."

"The potato chip factory? The Old Dutch?"

"That's what I said."

"Whose vehicle is that out in the driveway?" Ellie and Brand had walked past a dented green Toyota Corolla in the driveway on their way to the front door.

"Mine. Not exactly a limousine, is it?"

"What does Bill drive?"

"An F-150."

"Can you tell us what the plate number is?"

She shook her head. "I don't memorize that kind of stuff."

"What about you? Do you work?"

"Sure. I clean offices and washrooms at the university."

"Which building?"

"They move you around. You have to check the schedule for the week to know which one you're doing."

"Do you like your job?"

She snorted. "You're kidding, right? Who the hell would like cleaning toilets in a public building? It helps Bill pay the rent on this dump, like I said, and it puts some food on the table."

Ellie had been firing questions at her as quickly as possible, with hardly a breath in between, and Dawn had answered them just as fast. It was an interviewing technique she'd developed on her own while she was a constable on patrol, responding to calls. She used it when dealing with a subject whose veracity she doubted. While it was true that a pause between question and answer might indicate that the person was thinking up a lie, Ellie's theory was that when answers came too quickly, they'd likely been prepared by the person in advance to lead the interviewer—say, Ellie—down the garden path. This was what she was getting from Dawn, and she didn't like it.

"If you could help us," Ellie said, changing her tone, "we'd really appreciate it. We're trying to figure out how Cindy got from her place down to the entrance of the hiking trail where she was found. It's a distance of about fifteen kilometers. Do you have any idea at all who might have driven her there?"

Dawn shrugged elaborately. "Her father. If I had to guess."

"Anyone else come to mind?"

"Nope. I don't keep track of the kid's comings and goings."

"You didn't go up there to the house to pick her up for something?"

"I've already explained what I was doing on Saturday." She cocked her head. "Washer's done. If you'll excuse me, I'd like you to leave now so that I can get back to my laundry."

Out in the car, Ellie buckled up her seat belt with crisp, annoyed movements. "I don't like that woman. Something about her rubs me the wrong way."

Brand stopped at the nearest intersection and turned the corner. "What, exactly, rubs you the wrong way?"

"I don't know. She's just a bit too phony."

"Maybe she just gets nervous talking to authority figures," Brand said, his eyes on the traffic ahead of them.

"There's not a single nerve in that woman's body. *That* bothers me."

"Yeah," Brand said. "Yeah."

PRESENT DAY

The campus of the Canadian subsidiary of Trygram and Markson, maker of specialty chemicals and industrial minerals, was located on Highway 7 just west of Perth. As they rolled into the visitors' parking lot, Kevin and Heather ran their eyes over the newish collection of gray multi-storey buildings with their flat blue roofs and blue-tinted windows. It was a nice-looking place, clean and tidy. They parked and went inside.

They were shown to a waiting area from which Peter Gunsolus quickly retrieved them. After identifying themselves, they followed him to his office at the end of the corridor on the ground floor.

"Sit down, please. You want to talk to me about Alex's T-Bird, do you?"

His pot belly peeked up from the edge of his desk, round beneath a green golf shirt featuring a T&M logo, but his biceps and forearms were ripped, and his shoulders were broad. An athletic man gone to seed, gray strands shot through his faded tawny hair.

"That's right," Heather said. "According to your friend, you saw it involved in an accident on Dufferin Street on Saturday."

"That's right."

"What time of day was that, Mr. Gunsolus?"

"Pete. Lunch hour. Close to twelve thirty."

"Tell us what you saw, Pete."

"Sure." He leaned back in his chair and crossed his legs. White golf pants with a light pastel check; white golf shoes with blue softspikes on the soles.

"I was driving on Dufferin heading home after picking up some groceries. I saw the accident right out front of the McDonald's. Right away I thought it was Alex, but two men got out of the T-Bird. Never saw them before in my life."

"Do you still think it was his car?"

"You know what? I don't know. Sure looked like it, though. And I've never seen another black 1964 Thunderbird in this town, ever, and I've lived here for nearly forty years."

"Can you describe the two men?"

"I only saw them for a second," Gunsolus said, "and I had to watch the guy in front of me so I wouldn't rear-end him, but it's like a snapshot in my head."

Heather glanced at Kevin, who was taking notes.

"The guy who was driving was a little weasel type. Messy dark hair; black shirt with the sleeves rolled way up; sunglasses so you couldn't see his eyes. Looked like a little prick. The other guy was tall and fat—well, not quite fat but overweight, if I'm gonna be diplomatic about it. The goofball was wearing a black raincoat even though it was hotter than fucking hell—excuse the language. All dressed in black, and the sunglasses."

"What were they doing?"

He shrugged. "Getting out of their car. To talk to the other driver."

It occurred to Kevin that they didn't have any information about the other vehicle in the collision. If they could find this driver, he or she might serve as a useful witness in tracking down the two car thieves.

"What can you tell us about the other driver?" he asked.

"Not much. A woman. Middle-aged. Dark hair. By herself, looked like."

"What about her car?"

"One of those big black SUV things. Looked new."

"What was the woman wearing?"

Gunsolus thought for a moment. "Dunno. Wait. A sweater. I mean, in this heat."

"What colour?"

"Black and white squares. Like an unlined jacket more than a sweater, I guess. Something like you'd wear at the cottage."

Kevin could suddenly see it, hung up on the coat tree

in her office, unworn since the spring, not worth the bother to take home. He looked at Heather.

"Ellie!"

CHAPTER 22

The office of the manager of the McDonald's on Dufferin Street was an eight-by-six-foot shoebox with room enough for a desk, a chair, a filing cabinet, and space for one other person if they didn't mind standing. When Kevin and Heather identified themselves and explained why they wanted to talk to her, she took them out into the lobby, where they found a quiet spot at the back of the seating area.

"I'm Wanda Todmann. When did you say this accident took place?"

"Yesterday morning," Heather said. "During the noon hour. Right out front. A Tahoe driven by one of our people, Detective Inspector Eleanor March. Do you know her?"

Wanda shook her head. "Can't say I do. Anyway, lunch hour's a really busy time for us. Can't stop to chat. I was working drive-thru myself to keep it moving."

"The Tahoe was parked in your lot right after the

accident, and it stayed there overnight."

"Oh, yeah. One of the girls let me know, and I was going to call the police and have it towed, but you people showed up on your own this morning. I was surprised."

The first thing Heather had done was identify the Tahoe through its plates. She then called it in, requesting a tow that would take it two blocks to Ident's garage-cum-lab, and they gave it a visual once-over while they were waiting.

There was damage at the front on the driver's side that was consistent with a fender-bender. The headlight and turn signal were smashed. Ellie's trademark black handbag, which she used instead of a briefcase, sat on the passenger seat. It looked undisturbed.

Once the tow truck had arrived, they came inside to talk to Wanda.

When Heather described Ellie to her, her eyes lit up.

"You're talking about the Big Mac Lady! That's what I always call her, because that's all she orders. Well, sometimes fries with them, and sometimes not."

"Did she ever give you her name?"

Wanda shook her head. "Pays cash every time. Otherwise I would've peeked at the name on her card."

"So you're saying she came through yesterday while you were on drive-through?"

"Yes. Five Big Macs. I said, 'You must be extra hungry today!' She said, 'Three are for my dog.' I said, 'Must be a big dog,' and she said, 'He is.' That was it. I handed her her change and she drove off."

"Reggie," Kevin said. "The dog's name is Reggie. A German shepherd as big as a bear."

"I love big dogs," Wanda said. "The kind of dog you can throw your arms around and give a big hug."

"Sounds like you've got a dog yourself."

She laughed. "Alaskan Malamute. His name's Reacher. A big dog."

"How did she seem?" Heather asked. "What was her mood like?"

"Oh, she was tired. Very tired."

"Did she seem upset?"

"No more than usual. She doesn't seem like a very happy person to me. If you're saying she's a police detective, then I can understand why." She grimaced. "Sorry, no disrespect intended."

"None taken. Have you ever seen a black Thunderbird come through?"

"Thunderbird? You mean, like a vintage one? Can't say that I have. I can ask the kids. See if anyone knows about one."

"We'd appreciate that." Heather smiled. "Now, let's talk about video."

CHAPTER 23

Ellie slept most of Wednesday, drugged not only by the stuff they were giving her but also by the oppressive heat. She dreamt fitfully, random bits of movement and people that made no sense. She woke up parched, and found that someone had left a bottle of water on the floor next to her cot. It was tepid, but she drank it gratefully.

A few hours later, after the woman had taken her for a bathroom break, Junior came in with her supper on a paper plate—KFC chicken nuggets, fries, and a Pepsi.

When she'd cleaned it up, she put her head back on the pillow and closed her eyes.

"Dessert," Junior said.

She opened her eyes. He was holding out a mickey of Jack Daniel's whisky. She took it and drank a large mouthful, coughing at the back-kick of alcohol fumes that stung her nose.

"Thanks," she gasped. "How'd you know?"

"Know what?"

"Never mind." She filled her mouth again, swished it around, and swallowed it down.

Junior laughed. "Didn't take you for a drinker."

She handed him the bottle, with only a small amount left. "You never can tell." She thought, briefly, about the inadvisability of downing alcohol while her bloodstream was filled with whatever crap they were giving her to keep her docile, but she failed to summon up enough energy to give a damn.

He put the bottle away. "Bruno got to you, did he?"

"Oh, no." She put her head back and closed her eyes again. "He's very charming. Really."

That was good for another laugh. "He's a warped, mean-assed son of a bitch. That's what he is."

"Mmm."

"Are you going to sleep now, Eleanor?"

"Not yet. Just resting my eyes."

"How about a bedtime story?"

"Mmm. Sure." The drug that Junior had put in her Pepsi was beginning to take effect, but she knew now from experience that it would take a while to put her completely out.

"Once upon a time, in the slums of São Paulo, there was a little street rat who fell in love with race cars. This little punk kid, whose name was Bruno, loved to hang around

Interlagos. Do you know what that is? No? That was the Formula One track where all the legends of the day drove when they came to the city.

"Little Bruno ingratiated himself with all the big shots, whom he knew by sight from having seen their photographs in magazines and newspapers, and so when he was eleven, the great Emerson Fittipaldi took notice of him and told his crew to bring him on as a gofer. Bruno worked his little tail off, and when it was time for Fittipaldi to race in the Brazilian Grand Prix that was held every year in Jacerapaguá, the F1 track in Rio, they took Bruno with them. This was 1980."

"Mmm. I was eight that year. I think."

"Only three years younger than our lord and master. There you go. So little Bruno toured with the legend until one day he got into a big fight with the pit boss and they threw him out. He switched right away to the Nelson Piquet team, because he was a really good gofer and, like I say, worked his ass off for them. He toured with them all over the world in the 1980s, picking up some auto mechanic skills as he went along.

"How . . . do you know all this?"

"Are you kidding? He's a mythical hero, Eleanor. Everyone knows the story of Bruno Ribeiro. Anyway, don't interrupt. Where was I? Oh yes, Montreal. June 1988, the Canadian Grand Prix. He was twenty. Between test runs and trials, the pit crew let him drive the backup car around the track when it was quiet. This one time the crewman was drunk and Bruno was also over the limit. He drove too fast, missed a turn, and totalled the car."

"Too bad."

"Yes, Eleanor, it was. He was really hurt. A lot of broken bones. And a broken back. He's been paralyzed from the waist down ever since."

"Mmm."

"Are you falling asleep on me?"

"Not yet."

"Good. My story's not done yet. We've reached the part where Bruno was left behind. By the Nelson Piquet team, and by everyone else in the industry. No one would touch him after such a stupid play as that. When he was finally discharged from hospital, confined to a wheelchair, there was no one to meet him. He had nowhere to go."

"Tch. Poor guy."

"A charity for the disabled found him begging for change in the street. They took him under their wing. Set him up in a disabled-ready apartment and subsidized his course work and apprenticeship to become a licenced mechanic. After he got his papers, they even found him a job as a high school automotive mechanics instructor."

"Mmm. Why is he such a prick?"

"The booze, Eleanor. The booze. It's hard on everyone, but real hard on a young man stuck in a chair for the rest of his life. It didn't take long for him to get bitter and mean-spirited. He hated teaching and hated us kids. He hated everything. Except me, I guess. He was my teacher when I was sixteen."

"Is he going to kill me?"

"I don't know. I really don't know."

"Guess."

"Probably."

"Oh great. Thanks. Tell me more story. I like that better."

"You're barely conscious. I'm wasting a fine story on a woman who can't stay awake."

"Still awake."

"He quit teaching and found a job on the waterfront. Not an easy thing for a cripple in a chair, but he was tough and he'd made some tough friends along the way. They set him up in an office job and he learned the ins and outs real fast."

"Mob."

"That's right, Eleanor. The Mob. He worked for them for more than ten years, and when their boss got arrested for something and was put away, Bruno moved in. He ran the port for nearly twenty years, and completely changed the way they handled cars."

He stopped talking.

Ellie was snoring.

It was just as well. What she didn't know about stolen vehicles, the operation at the Port of Montreal, the containers shipped to Nigeria and Ghana and the United Arab Emirates, and Junior's role in all of it, the better.

As he left the room and locked the door behind him, he prayed to the spirit of his grandmother, long dead in Jamaica, that Bruno would let the woman live.

CHAPTER 24

The next morning, which was Thursday, Ellie was pulled out of bed by a woman and a man assigned to do the housekeeping in her room. They stood her in a corner while they changed the bedclothes, ran a vacuum cleaner around the floor, and wiped down the cot frame and doorknob with a cloth. Ellie watched, groggy from the sedative.

The woman took her to an employee bathroom, different from the one she'd been using up to now. The woman stripped her, pushed her into the shower, and handed her a small bottle of soap.

Ellie washed herself and turned off the water. The woman gave her a towel, and Ellie dried herself. The woman gave her a pair of coveralls, a white T-shirt, and underwear from new packages. Ellie put them on, slowly, her hand against the wall to maintain her balance.

She was taken back to the room and told to lie down on the bed. She did so. She heard the door close, after which there were only vague sounds coming from other parts of the building.

Would Junior show up with her breakfast? And more sedative? What a lovely thought. They'd find it in her blood work when they did the autopsy, no doubt.

This cheerful thought led to scraps of memories connected to autopsies other than her own. She remembered Kevin Walker's first one, how he ran outside and threw up in a snowbank. She followed him out and got him into her Crown Vic so she could start the engine and turn on the heater. He'd been bent over in the parking lot, half frozen.

He was fine after that.

Her thoughts strayed to her own first time. The autopsy was performed at the Guelph General Hospital, which had a different name now. She could remember the building, cement and red brick. Busy place. She couldn't remember what floor Pathology was on. She groped around for the name of the forensic pathologist. James. No, Jameson. Like the whisky. Dr. James Jameson. No, the other brother of Jesus. Dr. John Jameson. No, John was an apostle, not a brother.

She remembered the victim, of course. Parts assembled by Jameson for examination. Gruesome. Sad.

The Paige girl.

SEPTEMBER 2002

CHAPTER 25

"See this?"

Ellie took a step forward for a better look. Dr. Jameson was pointing at divots on the thigh of the body's right, disarticulated leg.

"Raccoons. Getting at the meat under the skin." He moved down the dissection table. "And here, where the foot used to be. See the mastication marks? Rats come out of nowhere and attack the joints. Even squirrels will get in on the action, focusing on the small bones such as you'd find in a hand or a foot, looking for calcium. The foot that's gone from this leg may be in somebody's burrow, dragged there to feed a family."

"Cause of death," Ellie prompted.

"Yes." Dr. Jameson led the way to the top of the table. "If you look at the stump of the neck, you can see blotch marks that are the aftermath of bruising. Two here in the middle, and several on each side under the temporomandibular joint—

"The what?"

"Sorry, the TMJ, the joint that connects the lower jaw to the skull."He pointed it out. "There are blotches consistent with fingers. Here, left hand, and here, on the other side, a right hand. The hyoid's gone, because whatever scavenged the head had started to clean out the neck stump, but we still have enough to determine that this person was a victim of manual strangulation. Perhaps it wasn't fatal, because the crushing blow the head suffered on impact with the rock would have killed her instantly anyway."

"Can you get us some fingerprints?"

He shook his head. "I wish. Any distinctive markings in the blotches have already faded away."

"So she was being strangled and she twisted free and was pushed over the cliff. Is that it?"

Dr. Jameson smiled faintly. "That's your job to find out, detective. I'm afraid I can't help you with that one."

As Ellie stared at the head with its torn flesh, empty eye sockets and freshly washed hair, she realized it didn't bother her. Her stomach was fine. The smells penetrating through her mask weren't upsetting her. The pathos of the whole thing, the horrible death of a young teenager and the desecration of her body by wild animals, no longer reached her emotions. She'd moved it all into a box at the back of her head where it would stay for a very long time.

This was Eleanor March at twenty-nine years of age.

As she lay on her cot in captivity, more than two decades later, Eleanor March wept hot tears for the lost soul that had been Cindy Paige.

PRESENT DAY

CHAPTER 26

"Who's the patron saint of surveillance?" Liam wanted to know.

Heather closed her eyes and made fists.

"St. Francis of a CCTV. What do you call worms you can see with your doorstep cam? Ring worms. What—"

"Liam."

"Yes, Heather."

"Would it be possible for you not to tell us any more jokes? Say, for the rest of the day? Or the rest of your life, even?"

Kevin watched the grin fall from Liam's face like a penny dropped down a well.

"Uh, sure, Heather. You don't like them?"

"No, it's not that. They're actually pretty hilarious."

He winced at her sarcasm. "Okay, okay. You don't have to hit me over the head. It's like yesterday a book fell and hit me on the head. I've only my shelf to blame." He threw up his hands. "Sorry! Last one, I swear."

Kevin said, "Alaric, we've been over and over this video—"

Everyone looked at Liam, who studied the ceiling with apparent interest in the stains and cracks.

"—and we're not getting anywhere."

"Sorry," Alaric replied, "these are all the streetcams available to us. Here," he pointed to one of several laptops in front of him, "I've got two weather-related ones open, but they don't see the section of Dufferin we want."

"Look at it," Heather said. "It's really raining out there now."

"Yeah. This one," he pointed to another laptop, "gives us the intersection at Wilson, but you can't see far enough up Dufferin from here, either."

"Damn," Heather muttered.

"The best I can do is what you've already seen—a black Thunderbird approaching Wilson Street on Dufferin westbound. Here, I'll run it again. There's the left-hand turn onto Wilson. I grabbed a still of the plate. It's Mr. Powell's car, all right."

"Great," Heather groused, "but they could be going anywhere."

"True," Liam said, "but if we assume they're heading for their cooling spot to stash it for a while, without making an ass of you and me, if you know what I mean, at least we know where the cooling spot isn't."

"That doesn't make any sense at all."

"No, come on, Heather. Think about it. They didn't go straight through the intersection, so their cooling spot's not somewhere west of here down Highway 7, like at Maberly or something, right?"

"Okay," she said grudgingly.

"And it's not north of here either, like maybe Lanark village or somewhere up there, because they didn't go through the intersection so they could turn north onto 511."

"And it's not east of here," added Kevin, "because they took the car west and then south."

Alaric snorted. "A fine bit of deduction, Watsons."

"Thanks. Now, wouldn't it make sense to start looking at warehouses in that direction instead of all over the place on the map?"

"Let me take care of that. Why don't you interview the other owners to see what they can add to the picture?"

Kevin said to Heather, "I've got something else to run down at the moment. Maybe you two guys can start with Mrs. Ledbetter."

"The Beemer lady," Liam said.

"Are you up for this?" Heather asked him.

"Of course. Why wouldn't I be?"

"And you'll can the corn?"

"I said I would, didn't I?"

Heather drove. From the passenger side, Liam looked

over his shoulder at the comic books scattered across the back seat.

"My hobby," she said. "What's yours?"

"Vinyl."

"Blow-up dolls? Why am I not surprised?"

He chuckled. "Records. LPs. Music."

"How many you got?"

"I'm not sure. Just one shelving unit."

"You haven't counted them?"

He shook his head, slipping on a pair of sunglasses. "I just do it by measurement. There are about seven LPs to an inch. The shelving unit has five shelves of three feet each, which is one hundred and eighty inches. Times seven is one thousand, two hundred and sixty albums. Give or take."

"So what kind of music do you listen to? Opera?"

Liam shrugged. "A bit of everything. I picked up a bunch of signed albums over the years from my parents' bar in T-Bay."

"Oh?"

"Yeah. Sam Roberts, his *Love at the End of the World.* Great Big Sea, *Fortune's Favour.* Tokyo Police Club, their first, *Elephant Shell.* Like that."

"Nice."

She stopped at a red light. "So, what was the deal with the Indian Posse guy?"

"You don't want to hear about that."

"Why not? Something to hide?"

"Of course not. It's all on the record, Heather. You're

just trying to bait me."

"I'm trying to find out your side of the story."

He sighed, turning away to look out the window. The light turned green and they rolled through the intersection.

"Not much to tell that I haven't already said. I got a tip that Donny Creeley was hanging out at a roadhouse just outside of town. I went out for a look and, sure enough, there he was."

"This is outside of North Bay."

"That's right. He'd relocated from Winnipeg to get away from a bunch of outstanding warrants, like for a couple of drive-bys and for drug trafficking, and he was starting up his own Posse chapter there in the Bay. Had already racked up a couple of assaults and so on. The usual stuff."

"So you walked right in and tapped him on the shoulder."

Liam laughed. "That's exactly what I did."

"Come on, you're shitting me."

"I shit you not. He was right there, sitting at the bar. Looked like he was by himself. Stool next to him was empty, so I slid in and tapped him on the shoulder. He was a little drunk."

"Big guy? Little guy?"

"About five-ten, but tough. No fat on him anywhere. Indigenous features but with a flattened nose and a lot of scars. And all the tatts."

"Weren't you pissing your pants?"

"Too much adrenaline, I guess, and not enough brains. I badged him and explained what was happening. He took it okay at first; finished his drink and stood up. Turned around so I could cuff him. As I was taking him out, a couple of guys got up from tables and closed in, but I put my hand on the butt of my Glock and they got the message. I got him out the front door and down the steps. Guys followed us out, and other people in the parking lot came up to see what was going on. Right then he twisted around and head-butted me."

"Ouch."

"I still had a hold of him, so I head-butted him back, and down he went. I bent over him and bam, he kicked me right between the legs. Just missed my package and caught me in the abdomen, right about where a hernia hurts the most."

Heather laughed.

"Only a woman could laugh about a guy getting kicked between the legs. Anyway, I fell on him and pounded him twice in the teeth to calm him down. By the time we finished rolling around, a cruiser had pulled into the lot to give me a hand."

"Sounds like you're a real tough guy."

Liam let it ride for a moment. Then he looked at her. "You don't seem to like me very much, Heather. I'm not sure why."

"No comment," she said, averting her eyes.

CHAPTER 27

As they walked into the reception area of Back Staircase Distillery, which was located at the far end of Rogers Road in Perth, Heather saw Liam's nostrils flare at the odour hanging in the air. She could smell it as well—the faint fragrance of apple pie. Not exactly what she'd expected in a place that made whisky, vodka, and gin.

"Jury's out," Liam murmured. "I'm not partial to flavoured spirits."

"Such a purist."

"Too sweet. People drink a lot, and then they throw up all over the place."

"I guess the answer to that is to not drink too much."

Mrs. Jane Ledbetter was waiting for them. She was a tall, fifties-something platinum blonde in an expensive-looking tan skirt suit. She led them through a security door and down a hallway to her office, a spacious room with a panoramic view of the back parking lot.

"We're distilling apple pie moonshine today," she said as they settled down and Liam took out his notebook. "Our 'Holler Apple Pie.' One of our best sellers."

"I'm surprised."

She smiled. "Our London-style gin is an award winner and our flagship spirit, yes, but moonshine has a very enthusiastic niche market and our apple pie mash bill hits the right notes for a lot of people."

Heather said, "Tell us about the theft of your car."

Her expression changed. "You know, I pride myself on my decision-making. That's how I built this company from the ground up. It used to be one of those brew-it-yourself places that was a fad for a while in the nineties. When it went under, I didn't hesitate. Bought it—lock, stock, and barrel. Right away I set it up for gin production. After a few trial runs, we came up with "Juniper Girl Dry Special" and never looked back. My point being, I've always been very good at making decisions, but choosing that damned storage place was a mistake."

"You're talking about Carson Storage," Heather said.

"Correct. I considered a lawsuit against them for negligence, but my lawyer looked at the contract I signed and they're covered. I know I read all the fine print; I just over-estimated the security they were guaranteeing."

"So the car that was stolen was a 1974 BMW, powder blue."

"Correct. The storage unit had an electronic lock on it. Let them explain how that was cracked with no apparent effort."

"How long have you had the car, Mrs. Ledbetter?"

"Seven years. I bought it to celebrate the launch of our 'Lanark's Best Sour Mash Whisky,' which became a money-maker right away."

"When was the last time you entered the unit?"

"I'm not sure. I decided not to drive the car this summer. Maybe three months ago?"

"Was the car kept locked?"

"Inside the unit? The so-called secure unit with the ultimate secure electronic locking system? No, but I'm sure that wouldn't have slowed them down. If they can get by the electronics, they can get by a 1974 car door lock."

"Did you ever let anyone into the unit other than yourself? Maybe a friend, to show it off, or a prospective buyer?"

"My friends aren't interested in cars, and I'm not interested in selling my Beemer. I *am* interested, though, in getting it back."

It's probably in Dubai by now, Heather thought, *so good luck with that.*

The manager of Carson Storage was a young guy, pleasant and polite. He sat behind a cluttered desk in a small office decorated with yellowed Toronto *Sun* sunshine girls who would now be in their fifties. Heather figured the guy who put them up in the first place would probably now be in his late seventies, if he was still on this side of the ground.

"So, Jimmy," she began, reading the name embroidered on his shirt, "we want to talk to you about Unit 437, the one that was leased by Mrs. Jane Ledbetter when her vintage Beemer was stolen."

"Sure. No problem. What would you like to know?"

"Explain your security system to us, will you?"

"Sure. No problem. It's an Impenetrable Sentinel 4.0 SmartLock, weather-resistant, tamper-proof, with wireless, contactless access to each unit."

"You sound like a sales brochure."

"Sorry. My Uncle Bob sells them."

"So, explain something. How did this wonderful wireless impenetrable lock get busted into without any apparent effort?"

"You know, that's a real good question. I'd like to know the answer, and so would Uncle Bob."

"Make a guess, Jimmy. Humour me."

"Uncle Bob says it must have been that she gave someone access to her digital key. So they could go in and look at it."

"She says not, Jimmy. Try again."

"Um. He did say—Uncle Bob, I mean—that there's a bunch of other ways to do it. Like, someone hacks her cellphone, steals the PIN next time she uses it, and gets in that way."

"She hasn't used it for at least three months. They wouldn't wait that long to steal a juicy ride like that. What else you got for me?"

"Uh, the smartlocks all use what's called Z-Wave, which is a wireless communications protocol common with programs that let you control your front door lock, your lights, thermostat and all that other stuff. You can just add our locks to your app as another device you can control on your cellphone."

"Okay. And?"

"Some apps have a bug in them that a hacker can use to reset the user codes. Then they can unlock the door whenever they want. Uncle Bob told his boss they'd better try to find this bug if it's there."

"Might be a good idea. Show us the unit now, would you?"

It was locked, of course. Jimmy showed them how to use the app to open it, assuring them that the PIN had been reset after Mrs. Ledbetter terminated the lease agreement. It was empty; not yet reassigned to another customer.

Heather sighed. Another case of closing the barn door after the horse was long gone.

CHAPTER 28

Carleton Place, in case you've never been there and might some day want to drop by and take a look for yourself, was a town of just over 12,000 souls. It was sort of a hub, with spokes running to Ottawa in the east, Smiths Falls to the southeast, Perth to the southwest, and about a million acres of rocky Canadian Shield to the west.

The Mississippi River ran through it, and while its name derived from the same Algonquin word as its American counterpart (*Misi-ziibi*, meaning "great river"), Kevin was not aware of any connection between it and the Mississippi River watershed running through the heart of the United States. In fact, this Mississippi was a tributary of the Ottawa River and, as such, shipped Canadian water down its length.

If you rode the current through the town and out the other end, say in a canoe or on a raft with a good friend named Jim, after twenty kilometers or so you'd reach a widening of the river, wide enough to rate being called a lake. Mississippi Lake, of course. Now you will have arrived in cottage country, with almost a thousand homes and seasonal properties around its rim. Not to mention campgrounds, resorts, and marinas within easy access to several restaurants with decent food and a beautiful view of the water.

Kevin parked in front of Charlie's Marina and Bait shop, which happened to be the largest marina on the lake. After drawing in a few lungfuls of lakeshore air, which smells like nothing else in the known universe, he went inside and showed his badge and warrant card to the guy behind the counter. A small, friendly-looking fellow, he was busily stocking a rotating display rack with bags of rubber worms.

"I didn't think you could still get those things," Kevin said. "I haven't seen them since I was a kid."

The man grinned, showing a gap between his front teeth. "I tell you what, you want an artificial bait that bass can't get enough of, these are your guys."

"I'll be darned. You Charlie?"

"Charlie's been dead for six years, son. I'm the owner. Walt Flood."

"Mr. Flood, I'm following up on the theft of this outboard motor." Kevin held up his cellphone, where he'd opened up Gerry Millen's photograph of his Merc. "It was stolen a few days ago from one of the cottages on the lake and was discovered missing on Monday. It's a Mercury 115."

"I can see that. Nice motor. I don't buy and sell hardware, though. Just live bait and these guys," he pointed a thumb at the rubber worms, which were in fact made of silicone, "and other stock from my wholesalers. On the shelves behind me. Chips, peanuts in the shell, pop, energy drinks. Convenience store stuff. Sunglasses; hats; T-shirts with our name on them. Plus boat covers and the like. No boats, though, and no motors."

"Have you heard any talk about one of these Mercs for sale in the past day or two?"

"Nope. Nice hat, by the way."

"Thanks." Kevin put his phone in his pocket and took out his notebook. "Does this sort of thing happen a lot on the lake? Break-ins and theft?"

"Oh, Christ, all the time. I'm surprised you'd ask."

"I don't spend a lot of time on property crimes," Kevin said, playing dumb. "I'm usually assigned to assault cases and that sort of thing."

Walt nodded. "You've got the size for it."

"How would someone dispose of something like that? Are there fences who handle boat engines?"

Walt narrowed his eyes. "I don't know much about it. I stay away from that kind of stuff. Sorry."

Kevin put his notebook away. "On another subject, I'm looking into a string of car thefts in the area. High-end stuff: sports cars, luxury vehicles, muscle cars. They keep them around here somewhere before shipping them off in containers out of Montreal. If you've heard anything, anything at all about that kind of operation, I'd really appreciate a word. Supposedly run by a guy named Bruno."

"Can't help you with that, but if I hear something, I'll let you know."

"Thanks," Kevin said, giving him a business card.

Walt looked at the card and opened his cash register. He lifted up the till, dropped the card in, and closed the drawer again. "Look, you seem like a nice enough guy. I'm not trying to play games. I keep my nose clean and the crooks usually leave me alone. I look the other way if something's being moved from one boat to another, know what I mean, but generally speaking I don't like illegal shit going on around here.

"There's a guy comes in every now and again to meet a boat that rents one of my slips. When the gate's open people can come and go, so this guy does exactly that. He drives a Dodge Ram and always unloads something onto this other guy's boat. Like I say, I don't get involved."

"Who rents the slip?"

"I'd rather not say, unless you force me to, but I seen that truck enough times that I can tell you the plate number on it. If you're looking for a stolen motor, that's the guy you might want to talk to."

Kevin retrieved his notebook and waited expectantly. Walt rattled off the licence number.

"Black Ram, looks pretty new. Guy's in his forties; shaved head; black T-shirts and jeans. Haven't a clue what his name is or where he lives."

"Thanks," Kevin said.

CHAPTER 29

When Kevin ran the plate, it gave him a hit on Ron Hayworth, born June 16, 1980, with an address on Carroll Road, north of Smiths Falls. A few other searches informed him that Hayworth was a bricklayer, currently employed by a Smiths Falls company called Jordan and Harsch Construction.

He made a quick men's room stop, and as he stood at the sinks washing his hands, Aydin Farzan walked in. Kevin waited until he was finished at the urinal and washing up beside him, before saying hello.

"Got something on the go right now?"

Farzan shook his head. "Just finished a report. Why?"

"I'm looking into an outboard motor theft and thought

I'd have a chat with a guy who may have taken it. A little company would be nice."

Farzan hesitated a moment before nodding. It was the first time Kevin had approached him, other than to give him a polite greeting and handshake when he first reported to the detachment, and the occasional hello in the lunch room or the parking lot.

Kevin took a few minutes to line up a patrol cruiser to accompany them, and then he and Farzan piled into Kevin's car and headed out.

"Do you play chess?" Farzan asked as they waited for a car ahead of them to make a left-hand turn.

Kevin shook his head. "Can't stand it. But I understand you're pretty good."

"I like the game."

"That's what Alaric tells me."

"He's an excellent opponent."

"So, do you like drug enforcement?"

"Yeah."

Traffic began to move again.

"It's where the action is," Farzan said. "And I don't like to see kids victimized like that. Before they know what's good for them."

"I hear you."

Farzan stared at him. "Before you ask, my parents came to Canada from Iran before I was born. They were escaping persecution as Christians."

"I wasn't going to ask."

"Sure you were. You were just trying to think of a way

to work it into the conversation."

Kevin laughed.

"I heard someone say your daughter's in first year at Carleton."

"Yeah, that's right."

"What's her major going to be?"

"Psychology."

"Mmm. I got my law degree there, with a minor in math. Good school."

"You were in Middlesex. How was it?"

Farzan shrugged. "Same as everywhere else."

He didn't seem inclined to offer up any further details, so Kevin let it ride and concentrated on his driving.

Hayworth's house was an old log home covered with clapboards that used to be painted white but were now the colour of road dust. The chimney was missing a few bricks, and the front verandah didn't look safe to walk on.

They walked past the black Dodge Ram with the appropriate licence plate number in the driveway and found Hayworth sitting in his back yard, drinking beer from a cooler and streaming a baseball game on his phone. Walt Flood's description had been pretty much on the money—a guy in his forties with a shaved head and a lantern jaw, a soiled black T-shirt with a Nirvana logo on it, stained jeans, and cowboy boots that hadn't seen polish so far this decade.

"A little buzzed," Farzan observed.

Kevin badged him, identifying himself and Farzan.

Hayworth drained his can of beer and popped another one.

"We're looking for a black Merc 115, Mr. Hayworth. Seen one around lately?"

"Ain't seen nothing lately, rooster. Beat it and let me watch the fucking game in peace."

Farzan wandered off, his cellphone out. Kevin had forwarded the photos to him. The back yard was littered with stuff. Three, no, four boats of different sizes on trailers; a Triton shipping container with its doors open; scrappy looking boat motors; miscellaneous parts like boat seats; gas tanks, canopies, and so on.

"I understand you're a bricklayer," Kevin said. "Who do you work for?"

"None of your fucking business, that's who." He said it quietly, without rancor.

"Dan Jordan, maybe?"

Hayworth said nothing, chugging his beer and tossing the empty can. He leaned back and fished another one out of the cooler, belching loudly.

Kevin saw Farzan standing in front of the open doors of the container. He was staring at him. Kevin raised his eyebrows. Farzan nodded.

"When's your friend due to show up at Charlie's?"

"Got no friends at Charlie's. Fucking A. Base hit." Cheers erupted from his cellphone.

Kevin strolled over to Farzan, who pointed with his chin at the open container doors. The damned motor was sitting right there on a home-made wooden stand.

Kevin knelt down to compare the identification plate with the photo on his phone. It was a match, all right.

As Kevin strolled back to arrest Hayward, the two constables who'd come with them stepped forward.

"Shit," one of them said.

Kevin turned.

A very large dog, a cross between a mastiff and a shepherd, appeared in front of Farzan. It looked like it weighed a hundred pounds. It crouched, growling, its teeth bared. As Kevin and the constables drew their weapons, Farzan whipped off his suit jacket and wrapped it around his forearm.

The dog leaped.

Farzan caught it on his arm. He staggered back but kept his balance. As the dog tried to rag-doll him, Farzan calmly drew his sidearm and struck the dog on the head just behind its ear, using the butt of the weapon like a club.

The dog sagged down onto the ground and lay still, taking the jacket with him. Farzan freed himself and re-holstered his gun.

"Brutus!" Hayward shouted, jumping to his feet. "You son of a bitch raghead! You fucking killed him!"

Farzan grinned. "Nah. Still breathing. He'll wake up in the shelter with a real bad headache, though."

CHAPTER 30

"What day is it?"

"Thursday," Junior told her. "Finish your hotdog."

Ellie slowly complied. "How long are you going to keep me here?"

"I don't know."

Hotdog done, Ellie put her head back on the pillow and closed her eyes. Seemingly for the millionth time. "I want to get out of here."

"I know. I'm sorry, Eleanor."

"Sure."

He left, and she lay there quietly. Nice guy, but it's still kidnapping. He'll have to pay the price, just like the others. What's-his-name in the wheelchair, and goddamned Squid, and Bathroom Lady, and all the rest of them.

Section 279, *Criminal Code*: "Kidnapping, Trafficking in Persons, Hostage Taking and Abduction." She'd dealt with it before. She'd even written an essay on it once. When was that again? Grade . . . Ten. Yeah. The Contemporary Canada course, which had a module on Canadian law.

Why the hell had she written an essay on something like that? She had to think about it. Right. The Christopher Stephenson kidnapping. An eleven-year-old taken from a shopping mall in Brampton, only forty-five kilometers northwest of where she lived. Sexually assaulted and murdered. The crime eventually resulted in Christopher's Law, which mandated the creation of the OPP's Ontario Sex Offenders Registry, long after the fact. At the time, young Ellie had used her essay to express her frustration at the lack of safety for children in public places, and she'd called on law enforcement and the justice system to do something about it.

As a high school student, she'd emerged somewhat from her shell, participating in some extra-curricular activities and speaking up in class. She'd chosen the four-year commercial program, rather than the university-track option, thinking the business courses would please Paul and Mary. The courses were remedial, and she had very little difficulty scoring high marks across the board. Typing, accounting, business correspondence. Not much of a challenge for her.

She remembered, though, why she suddenly became so personally interested in the law. The *Code* in particular.

This was Eleanor March at fifteen years of age.

She was home from school because it was a profess-ional development day for the teachers. She was in Grade Ten, and her favourite course was Phys Ed. She played on the basketball team and the badminton team. She remembered, vaguely, telling Kevin Walker once that she disliked athletics. As a girl, though, she'd loved it.

It was 1991, late April, a Friday. Paul opened the store at ten. Ellie brought down a cup of coffee for him at 10:15 or so. Mary followed with a small plate of *lakotki*, buttery shortbread cookies that Paul loved to nibble with his coffee in the morning. Mary brought tea for herself and for Ellie.

The clock dipped to 10:30 AM and the first customer had yet to arrive. A light rain fell in the street outside, which might have explained how quiet it was. Paul and Mary chatted in Polish; Ellie listened, never having learned the language but liking the sound of their voices. She watched scraps of paper getting plastered on the sidewalk by the rain.

In some towns, it might be fallen leaves. On Yonge Street, it was litter. Handbills; advertising flyers; junk mail.

The shop door opened and two men entered. One wore a balaclava and the other a kerchief over his nose and mouth. They both carried guns.

Balaclava strode up to the little counter where Paul and Mary sat. He waved the gun at their noses.

"This is a robbery, get it? Open the register and hand over all the money."

"Yes," Paul replied, putting down his coffee. "I thought it might be, given the guns and disguises, but wouldn't there be more money in the till at the end of the day instead of the beginning?"

Balaclava cut him across the mouth with the barrel of his gun, knocking him off his stool. Mary screamed, dropping to her knees beside him.

Ellie made a move toward Balaclava but Kerchief, covering the door, pointed his gun at her. "Don't."

Anger spiked in her, but she fought it down.

"Let me do it," she said, moving to the cash register. She opened the till. "Do you have a bag?"

Balaclava thrust a canvas bag at her. "Watch your mouth, or you'll get what he got."

As she took the bag, she noticed the cuff of his jacket pulling up over his black leather gloves to reveal the top of a tattoo on the back of his hand. It was a rectangular shape on a diagonal. She figured it was probably the top of a swastika.

His eyes, seen through the openings in the balaclava, were blue. His eyebrows were the colour of straw. His voice was a smooth tenor, without nervousness or an accent.

She filled the bag with the cash in the till, which was the sum total of Paul's $200 float for the morning.

"What else?" demanded Balaclava.

"That's it. Paul's right; you picked the wrong time of day."

He swore, threatened her with the gun, and stomped out into the rain, followed by his partner. They turned left, heading north up Yonge Street.

She checked on Paul. He was sitting up. Mary wiped blood from his face with a hand towel from under the counter. Paul caught Ellie's eye and nodded.

She locked the front door and looked down at the footprints on the floor. The sneakers that Kerchief had worn had left only a smudge, but several wet imprints left behind by Balaclava told her that treads on the soles of his boots included swastikas and lightning bolts. A white supremacist, apparently.

She found an empty shoe box and placed it over the best impression to protect it for the police. She helped Mary get Paul to his feet and up onto his stool.

"I hate getting robbed," he mumbled.

Ellie called 911 from the phone next to the cash register.

SEPTEMBER 2002

CHAPTER 31

Madison McEwen was a likeable kid, bright and polite, but at the moment she was scared to death as she came into the living room and sat down opposite Ellie and Brand. She flicked her long, black hair from her eyes and tried to smile, but it didn't work.

"I'm Detective Constable Eleanor March, and this is Detective Constable Brand. We'd like to talk to you about Cindy Paige."

"All right."

"You were friends at Stephen G. McQueen Public School, were you?"

"Yes."

"And you graduated together this year?"

"Yes."

"And now you're both at Fergus High, right?"

"Yes."

"How do you feel about that? Changing schools, stepping up into a bigger place with more kids and different teachers?"

"All right, I guess."

"How did Cindy feel about it?"

A tiny smile. "Excited. She always liked new adventures."

A tear rolled down her cheek. Brand reached into his jacket pocket and handed the girl a small, unopened package of tissues. She fumbled at it for a moment before her mother took it from her, opened it, and gave her one.

As Ellie queued up her next questions, she filed that small gesture away for future reference. It had never occurred to her at any point to have tissues handy when interviewing someone. From now on, it would.

"What kind of adventures did Cindy like, Madison?"

"Oh, she loved hiking, especially on new trails. Last winter she tried skiing for the first time. I lent her my equipment. She tried out for the basketball team and actually made the junior girls."

"How were her grades?"

"Mostly Bs and B-plusses. She wasn't all that good at studying."

"But you're a straight-A student."

"Yes."

"Did you help her with homework sometimes?"

A nod.

"How did she get along with the other kids?"

"Okay." A glance at her mother. "There's some hazing, because we're frosh, but you try to ignore it."

"Any particular kids?"

"A couple of Grade Elevens."

"Any particular kids who might have been her enemy?"

"No."

"Did the hazing bother Cindy?"

"Not very much. She was good enough at basketball that they mostly left her alone."

"Your mom tells us you're good at art and photography."

Madison nodded, blushing.

"Do you have any pictures of Cindy we could look at?"

"Sure. The album's up in my room." She glanced at her mother, who nodded.

While they waited, Brand cleared his throat. "Mrs. McEwen , how did Cindy seem to you?"

"You mean in general? She was a nice girl. Quiet, but not too happy, I thought."

"What gave you that impression?"

"I'm not quite sure. Just a feeling that things weren't going well for her."

"At home?"

"I don't know. I didn't know her all that well."

Ellie listened to the cultured tones in Mrs. McEwen's voice. "What do you and your husband do for a living?"

"We're at the university. Ian teaches Agricultural

Economics, and I teach English." She smiled. "My specialty's Chaucer, but that never seems to show up on the reading lists. Not even my books on the subject, unfortunately. But I'm also pretty good at Shakespeare, so we cover that."

"You and your husband prefer small-town Fergus to the city, do you?"

"Yes. Madison's doing well up here, and the commute's not too bad, although you have to be careful in winter. Like anywhere else, I guess."

"Did you or your husband ever give Cindy rides anywhere? By herself?"

"No, never. A few times with Madison, but not alone. Why? Has her father said something?"

Madison had arrived with her photo album. She handed it to Ellie and knelt beside her, watching Ellie turn the pages slowly.

There were several photos of Cindy. Some were selfies of the two of them taken by Madison, while others were portraits: full-length; head-and-shoulders; and a few where Cindy posed against a limestone wall at some historical building in town.

Ellie pointed at a picture of Cindy with a boy who looked to be the same age.

"That's Robert," Meredith said. "He and Cindy were friends."

"Boyfriend and girlfriend?"

"Yeah, I guess. Sort of."

Ellie smiled. "Just sort of?"

"Well, he and I are friends, too." She glanced at her

mother, cheeks red.

"What's his last name?"

"Starr. Robert Starr."

"What kind of boy is he?"

"Nice. Smart. He's good at art, like me. Maybe better, even."

"Did they date?"

"Sometimes."

"Were you jealous of her?"

"Really, detective." Mrs. McEwen stirred restlessly. "Are you trying to upset her?"

"Please answer my question, Madison."

"Sometimes, a little bit, I guess. But I'm not that stuck on Robert. And he wasn't all that stuck on Cindy."

"It didn't interfere with your friendship with her? Robert in the middle?"

She shook her head. "Cindy and I got along real well. When you're first-year, you don't have a lot of friends. Everybody's looking out for themselves. But Cindy and I stuck together."

"All right, Madison. That's fine. Just a couple more questions and we're done. Did Cindy ever talk about her step-mom?"

"A few times when she was upset. She didn't like her."

"Why not?"

"I think she thought she was too phony. You know, that sing-songy voice adults use when they're being condescending."

"Did you ever meet her?"

"No, thankfully."

"What about other family?"

"She never talked about any."

"How about her father? Did she get along with him?"

A smile. "She was a daddy's girl. I mean that in a nice way. She really wanted to make him happy. At McQueen he'd come out to all her basketball games. He was always there in the bleachers, cheering for her. It was nice."

"What about her teachers? At Fergus, I mean."

She thought for a moment. "We were too new to know many of them. The ones teaching Grade Nine seemed to be okay, I guess." Madison paused. "She didn't like her basketball coach. Called her Miss Trunchbull."

Ellie smiled. "What's her real name?"

"Mrs. Gordon."

Ellie glanced at Brand, who shook his head microscopically. "Thanks very much, Meredith. You've been a great help. We really appreciate it."

The girl surprised her by standing up and shaking her hand, and then Brand's.

They did the honours with Mrs. McEwen and, on the way to the door, Madison put her hand on Ellie's arm.

"What really happened to her? Was it an accident, or did someone do it to her?"

"That's what we're trying to find out," Ellie replied, careful not to make any promises this time.

"If someone did it to her, find out who it was and punish them. She didn't deserve to die."

"No, she didn't."

CHAPTER 32

In the car, Brand gave her a look that said, "Good job" without actually having to utter the words.

"So, which one will we do first?" Ellie asked as they drove away. "The coach or the boyfriend?"

Brand grunted. "Coach first. You take her, and I'll take the kid."

As he drove, he glanced over at her. "Have you been following Bill 128?"

"No. What's that?"

"Jesus, Eleanor. Don't you think it would behoove you

to stay in touch with things that will have a permanent effect on your fellow officers?"

"Sure, but I still don't know what Bill 128 is."

"The *Highway Memorials for Fallen Police Officers Act*, Eleanor. They're going to start dedicating bridges and overpasses to the memory of those of us who are killed in the line of duty."

"Oh. I hadn't heard about that."

He snorted. "You have now. It's supposed to get royal assent in December. Start paying attention to it, will you?"

"Sure, Leif. No problem."

Fergus District High School was a squat, three-storey hulk designed in what was known as the collegiate gothic style of architecture, very popular for schools, colleges, armories, and, well, a lot more schools. It featured cut stone blocks, copper trim, and an extended front entrance framed by two short towers. Now seventy-five years old, it would have only two more years of active use before being replaced by a new building that wasn't quite as old and cold.

They found the principal's office and identified themselves, asking to see Mrs. Gordon. The secretary, a pleasant-looking middle-aged woman, fired up the public address system and paged her.

While they waited, Brand asked if the principal was in. The secretary, whose name was Margaret Allen, explained that Mr. Pulkinghorn was at a doctor's appointment.

"We also want to talk to one of the students, Robert Starr. Can you call his parents and see if one of them can come in?"

"Certainly. Is there some kind of trouble?"

"We just need to talk to him."

Margaret put through the call to the Starr residence, but it went straight to voicemail. She left a message.

A teacher walked in to check his mail in the big pigeon-hole message box on the far wall. Flicking through a couple of manila interoffice envelopes, he strolled over, hoping to pass the time of day with Margaret before wandering off again.

"These are police detectives who want to talk to Robert Starr," Mary said.

"Oh? Is there a problem?"

Brand asked, "Who are you?"

"I'm Greg Hamilton. History. And you are?"

"Detective Constable Brand. This is Detective Constable March." He didn't bother bringing out his badge again, so Ellie left hers in her pocket.

"Brand, eh? Are you Old Norse Brand or German Brand?"

"What kind of kid is Robert?" Brand asked, ignoring the man's genealogical probe.

Hamilton shrugged. "Seems like a very good student. I'm still getting to know the Grade Nines."

"What about Cindy Paige?"

Enlightenment dawned behind Hamilton's eyes. "Ahh. I see. Paige. We've only had one assignment so far, but I thought hers was fair to good."

A stout, middle-aged woman strolled into the office, eating a hotdog smothered in the fixings. Clutched in her other hand was a can of Dr. Pepper with a plastic straw sticking out. She swallowed a masticated ball of wiener, bun, relish, onions, ketchup, mustard, and crumbled potato chips, washed it down with a long pull on her soft drink, and wiped her mouth with the back of her hand.

"What do you want, Allen?"

Ellie instantly understood why Cindy Paige had called the woman "Miss Trunchbull."

"We have a few questions for you," Brand said, pulling out his badge this time. "Maybe we can use Mr. Pulkinghorn's office?"

"Mr. MacDougall's might be better," Margaret Allen said. "He's also away today."

"Whatever," Gordon snapped. "I'll try not to steal his pens."

Inside the office, Gordon closed the door and sat down behind the vice-principal's desk.

"What's this all about, anyway? I've got a lot of work to do."

"We're investigating the death of one of your student athletes," Ellie said. "We need to ask you a few questions."

"Ohh, sure. The Paige kid." She took another bite of her hotdog, spilling relish and chopped onions on Mr. MacDougall's desk.

"You were her basketball coach, correct?"

"Yeah, but she made the junior team only because we're short of athletes this year. Mediocre talent at best."

"What position did she play?"

"I had her coming off the bench as a reserve shooting guard. She was decent from the perimeter but overall, inconsistent." She popped the butt end of her hotdog into her mouth and swallowed it whole.

"Did you have any problems with her?"

"I found her a little sulky, if you want to know. She didn't like to be taken off the floor. She took everything personally. I don't like girls like that. I like girls who are mature and understand the nuances of the game."

"She was only a freshman," Ellie said.

"You obviously don't understand the sport."

"I remember when I was a frosh at Jarvis Collegiate. That's the one in Toronto. I was a point guard and pretty nervous, so I made mistakes, but in my senior year we won the championship and I led the division in scoring. You never know how a girl might turn out."

Gordon frowned, wiping her fingers on a serviette she'd used to hold the hotdog. "Well, I don't know about that. I just know she didn't make much of an impression."

"Did she have any problems with anyone on the team?"

"Not that I noticed."

Ellie handed her a card. "If you think of anything to add, give us a call."

Gordon took it with a sour look and walked out.

Brand leaned out and said to Margaret Allen, "We

want to talk to Robert Starr now. Were you able to reach his parents?"

"No, sorry."

"We'll need you to sit in on the interview. As a supervisory adult."

"Sure, I guess. Do you want me to page him now?"

"Please."

While they were waiting, Ellie said, "Mrs. Gordon seems like quite a prize."

"The kids hate her. She's a basket of sour grapes."

"Why doesn't the school get rid of her? Bring someone good in?"

Margaret looked unhappy. "She has a lot of friends on the board and in town. We all walk on eggshells around her."

"What was that bit about stealing his pens?"

Margaret rolled her eyes. "Mr. MacDougall's a bit of a fusspot. Pens kept disappearing from his desk. He had the whole school notified that the person caught stealing them would be punished. For whatever reason, he decided that Mrs. Gordon was the one who was taking them. They had a big argument in the teachers' lounge about it. She threw a can of pop at him but thankfully missed."

Brand laughed.

"Turned out he kept putting them in his briefcase at the end of the day and forgetting about them. There were more than a dozen in there when he finally got around to checking for them."

"Sounds like an idiot."

"He's okay. Just a bit of a persnickety old woman about things."

Brand eased his haunch onto the corner of her desk. "What do you know about Cindy Paige? Was she ever called into the office? What was your impression of her?"

"We have an enrollment of 484 students," Margaret said. "Over a hundred of those this year are freshmen. If they don't stand out for some reason really good or really bad, staff tend to overlook them in their first year. I don't think I would have recognized her if I saw her."

There was a noise in the doorway. A boy stood there, listening.

"Are you Robert Starr?" Brand asked.

"Yes."

"I'm Mr. Brand, and this is Ms. March. Let's go in here and talk for a minute."

"It's okay, Robert," Margaret said. "I'll come in and sit with you."

Great, Ellie thought. *Another scared-to-death kid.*

Brand motioned Margaret to take Mr. MacDougall's chair and for Robert to sit with him in front of the desk. Ellie faded into the background, leaning against a filing cabinet. Brand turned his chair to face the boy and crossed his legs informally, trying to set a casual tone.

"We're police detectives investigating the death of Cindy Paige, Robert. We're hoping you might know a few things about her that will help us."

"All right."

"You were friends with her, right?"

"Yeah."

"One of her friends showed us a picture of you and Cindy together. It looked like you got along well."

"Yeah, we did. She was pretty cool." He hesitated. "That must have been Madison."

Brand smiled. "Yeah, it was. So, was Cindy your girlfriend?"

Robert bit his lip. "Not really. We were good friends, but I wouldn't call her my girlfriend."

"Madison?"

He looked down, his cheeks red. "We have a lot more in common."

"But you also hung around with Cindy, right? What did you do together? Hiking?"

"No, we usually met at the library and went to Dairy Queen or something."

"Did she have any enemies? Girls jealous of her for some reason?"

He shook his head. "She kept a pretty low profile at school. Didn't talk much in class."

"Did you ever see her getting into a car with someone?"

"You mean, like her dad?"

"Other people. Older men, maybe. Someone you didn't know."

"No."

"What about your parents, Robert? Did they like Cindy?"

"I guess. They didn't really know her much."

"Did they ever give her rides anywhere? Maybe your dad? Would Cindy call him up and ask for a lift somewhere?"

"No. I—I'm going to be sick."

Margaret Allen grabbed Mr. MacDougall's wastepaper basket and brought it around the desk. Robert leaned forward and vomited into it.

"I think that's enough," she told Brand.

PRESENT DAY

Miss Judith Smith was a rather wealthy woman. As vice president of Finance and Corporate Services, and chief financial officer of the Perth and Smiths Falls District Hospital, she pulled down an annual salary of more than $185,000 plus benefits, according to the Ontario Sunshine List. Heather had checked out of curiosity while Liam drove them to the hospital on Drummond St. East.

According to LinkedIn, she'd been in the position for six years, before which she'd put in eighteen at the Queensway Carleton Hospital as Director of Finance and three years before that as office manager at a veterinarian hospital in Ottawa.

At this point in her career, Heather had dealt with a number of rich women, married and single, young and old, and she'd found a way to depersonalize the experience each time. They were almost always beautiful, while she was plumpish and plain. They were almost always married to handsome zillionaires, whereas she was a young widow who was careful with her money. They almost always spent their winters in warm places like Costa Rica, Madeira, or Bali, while she spent her winters in her car, freezing her ass off on stakeouts or getting stuck on back roads, caught in a snowstorm with all-season tires that had too little tread left on them.

But she'd learned to depersonalize it. Rich women had their own problems, too. What they were she wasn't quite sure, not being wealthy herself, but she could imagine they could get pretty serious, like an infected splinter or a turned ankle.

Her mind, therefore, was at ease as they followed coloured arrows on the floor to the administrative wing, where Miss Smith waited for them with coffee and a bright smile.

"Thank you for seeing us," Liam said, taking a seat across from her desk and crossing his long legs. "What a beautiful office you have."

"Thank you. My sister-in-law helped me decorate it. She has much better taste than I do."

It was a gorgeous office, Heather had to admit. Certainly a far cry from anything you'd see in law enforcement. She'd never enjoyed the experience of stepping into the commissioner's office before, and had no actual desire to do so, but she'd be willing to bet that it was nowhere near as nice as this one.

"As I mentioned on the phone," she began, "we want to go over a few things again regarding your stolen car."

"Of course. Is there any news?"

"No, but we're actively working on it, which is why Detective Constable Woolfson and I are here."

"Liam," he murmured.

"What can I help you with?"

"Your vehicle is a 2023 Audi A3, correct?"

"Yes. It only had 646 kilometers on it when I bought it for $45,000. Not an exorbitant purchase, and a good value for the money."

"And it was stolen from here, at the hospital. Is that correct?"

"Yes, unfortunately. I was very upset."

"How does that happen? Isn't there video surveillance of the parking lots here?"

She nodded. "Unfortunately, though, it was a very busy day and I ended up parking in a blind spot. The video saw the car leaving the lot, but that was all."

"Keyless entry, right?"

"Yes. I assume someone was able to capture the digital signal from my key fob and relay it to someone at the car waiting for it. These things have a fairly short range. The car thinks it's the genuine signal, and that's it."

"Where did you have your fob?"

"In my purse. Which I keep here in my office with me, locked in the desk drawer in case I have to leave the room. Ironically, I'd ordered a Faraday bag from Temu to keep the fob in. It's supposed to block the signal. It arrived two days after the theft. Not their fault, of course. Just frustrating."

"The day the car was stolen, did you have your purse with you somewhere?"

She thought. "Probably. I sometimes buy lunch in the cafeteria, and I'd have it with me then."

"Did you notice anyone unusual or out of place in the days before the theft, or that particular day?"

"This is a public building, detective. You'd be surprised at some of the strange types you see around here. Poor souls. Some real weirdos."

"No one stood out to you in any way?"

"It was almost three weeks ago, now. I can't remember— oh wait." She laughed. "That must have been the day I saw Oliver."

"Oliver?"

"I remember passing a man coming out of the cafeteria. It was a bit crowded and we bumped shoulders. I remember it because I thought he looked like the Canadian actor who played in *The West Wing* and *Chicago Med*. You know, Oliver Platt. I happen to like that actor and came within an ace of asking him what he was doing in Perth. Anyway, that's the only person I can think of."

"About how old?"

"Oh, mid-thirties. Dark hair."

"Height and weight?"

"Medium height, only an inch or two taller than I am; a little pudgy. He wore a black trench coat over a black polo shirt and black denim jeans. He had sunglasses on, the big aviator style, which I thought was a little odd for indoors."

"You have a pretty good memory," Liam said.

"Well, I've always liked Oliver Platt."

Back at the detachment office, they met with Alaric and ran through what they'd learned from the interviews. Heather wanted to point out that nearly none of these details could be found in Doug Skelton's files, but she bit her tongue.

After listening to them talk about the three cases—Alex Powell and his black Thunderbird; Jane Ledbetter and her Beemer; and Judith Smith and her Audi—Alaric offered a partial analysis.

"A team of two, seen with Powell's Thunderbird at the McDonald's fender bender and inferred with the theft of Smith's Audi. One guy looks like Oliver Platt auditioning for *The Matrix*. He's Mr. Inside. And the other is likely the driver. Mr. Outside. The one receiving the electronic signal from Mr. Inside and using it to start the car. I'd be willing to bet that Mr. Inside is the one with the skill set for electronic boosting."

"But not just a team of two," Liam suggested. "An organization, isn't it? They have a cooling spot; they containerize the cars and ship them to Montreal; they probably chop up less valuable vehicles and ship the parts. We're talking about an organized car theft ring on a pretty decent scale."

"I agree. I'll work that angle, and you two continue to

concentrate on these two guys. Does it look like they have a shopping list, or do they just pick out high-end targets when they see them? Do they scout target vehicles in advance? If so, people will have seen them."

"Not if you're talking about the dopes on Sheppard Avenue," Heather said, thinking of the canvass she and Kevin had conducted after interviewing Alex Powell. "A herd of elephants could parade down that street and they'd never notice."

Alaric smiled. "Anyway, let's get a warrant for the hospital video, say, going back a week before the theft. Let's see if we can spot their advance work."

"If it exists," she said.

"If it exists."

CHAPTER 34

Alaric Quinn was an easy-going kind of a guy, a dishevelled and shaggy young bear who wore ill-fitting clothes and sported black-framed glasses, a beard that he occasionally forgot to trim as per OPP policy, and Birkenstock clogs that Sonja Freeling preferred to ignore, knowing that her friend's feet were not in the best of shape.

Today was not one of his better days. As he'd told Liam earlier, his knee was bothering him because of the weather, and the pain was wearing away at his normally sunny disposition. The kratom helped, as an analgesic, but an undercurrent of discomfort remained, like a bass drone in a Bach composition.

It was something he'd lived with for more than twenty

years. Such a stupid thing, typical Alaric Quinn bad luck, but there was nothing to be done about it except shake his head at the memory.

He was fifteen. It was early August. He was stretched out on a lawn chair in the back yard, reading a book. He could still remember what it was: *Cybernetics* by Norbert Wiener, loaned to him by his computer science teacher, Mrs. Witchell. Engrossed, he'd only faintly registered the barking of his Jack Russell, Sparky, coming from the front step.

It was the sound of a car horn that got his attention. Sparky was a car chaser, and when he was put outside he was secured to a chain that he was able to stretch almost to the sidewalk but not beyond. This was trouble! He could hear the dog running back and forth, raising a racket, and cars slowing down to avoid flattening him.

"Sparky!" he shouted, reaching the low picket fence enclosing the back yard. "House, Sparky! House!"

The dog stopped on the sidewalk, looking back at him. He'd slipped his collar and was reveling in his newly found freedom.

"Sparky!" Alaric rushed to the gate, but it wouldn't open. His father had installed some recently invented latch system, but it wasn't working properly. There was nothing for it but to climb the fence before the bone-headed dog ended up getting hit by a car.

He was half-way over when the leg of his shorts snagged on a picket. He lost his balance and fell forward into his mother's little garden on the other side of the fence.

She liked bordering things with river rocks picked up on their weekend drives to the country—pink granite; basalt; limestone; quartzite. He didn't see which one he landed on—he only felt the impact and saw a bright flash as agony ripped through him.

He lay crumpled on the ground between a peony bush and a hydrangea, holding his knee. An x-ray would reveal that his patella had cracked into two pieces. There was nothing more painful, he decided later, than a broken kneecap.

Concerned, Sparky trotted over and began licking his face.

Such a good dog.

No, you could only shake your head at such a dopey memory.

In the comm room with him was Simon O'Connor, their civilian data entry assistant. In his mid-thirties, Simon wore his long, frizzy black hair pulled back in a ponytail to accommodate his headset. His fingers flew over the keyboard, his eyes on the screen in front of him.

Alaric's gaze dropped to Simon's feet. Today he was wearing burnt-orange Skechers, slip-ins with a mesh upper and heel pads for extra comfort. Tomorrow it would be something else. Simon was a shoe guy. He probably had more than fifty pairs, Alaric figured.

The subject of footwear made him instantly think of his father, of course. Pat Quinn had recently retired after more than twenty-five years as a high school shop teacher, but Alaric knew he wouldn't give up his home-based job until he keeled over dead at his workbench in the garage. The garage that hadn't seen a vehicle inside for as long as Alaric could remember.

Pat was a tinkerer, a technologist, a breadboard-and-gears man—an inventor. He held numerous patents for all kinds of stuff, including innovative solar panels, kitchen gadgets, green energy devices, exercise and hiking gear, and many other things, some very useful, some not so much.

Pat had spent the last six months trying to invent a pair of sneakers that could climb up the side of a wall—brick or stone, initially. He'd experimented with adhesives, tiny hooks like Velcro, even magnetism. There were a lot of examples of wearable technology already on the market as far as footwear went, but they mostly focused on medical devices and sensors for athletes and patients.

After half a year, he gave up on trying to emulate Spider-Man and switched to Maxwell Smart, Secret Agent 86 of CONTROL. In three months he developed a workable prototype of a Bluetooth-enabled shoe phone for which he was able to secure a patent. Rather than having to remove the shoe and hold to one's ear, as Max had comically done in the TV series *Get Smart*, a user could wear a headset to activate the phone and send and receive calls through voice command. Its main advantage, as he'd stated in his application, was that a person wouldn't have to carry around a cellphone; it was right there in their shoe.

Now he was unsuccessfully trying to license it to a shoe manufacturer for production. Unfortunately, everyone he'd talked to so far had laughed so hard he couldn't keep their attention long enough to finish his sales pitch.

While waiting for lightning to strike, he'd moved on to heads-up displays for automobiles. He was currently working on a model that would project information into the space between the driver and the windshield. It would be transparent, of course, and wireless, using Bluetooth to send information from a simple app added to the car's computer to a small device that could be stuck to the dash. It could easily be turned off and on, and the holographic display was supposed to be visible through polarized sunglasses and prescription eyewear. There were a number of such devices already on the market, and Pat had studied them carefully, finding design gaps and shortcomings he thought he could exploit in his invention.

Alaric had unwisely volunteered to test a prototype. The first few iterations had bugs in them that nearly drove him nuts, but Pat was slowly but surely smoothing things out. Maybe once it was patented, Alaric would keep one in his car. Maybe.

Alaric's personal cellphone began to vibrate. He looked at the call display and walked into an adjoining storage room where he turned on the light, closed the door, and sat down on a pallet of photocopy paper.

"Hey, Brooke. What's up?"

"Business first," a light feminine voice whispered in his ear, "then pleasure later."

"I love you, too. Did you find out anything?"

"Nothing that's going to make your day. Here's the

layout. You're bumping into something called Operation Cobalt Strike, an RCMP JFO with CBSA, the Sûreté du Québec, Montreal police, the Port Authority, and you guys."

"A dog's breakfast."

"Hey, we always run a tight ship. Anyway, since I started asking Bill a lot of questions, I've been designated as your contact. Your official OPP man on the job is a guy named Detective Sergeant Gilles Savard. Know him?"

"Slightly. He was in Ottawa when I was there."

"Yeah, well, you need to copy him on any information you pass along to me."

"Will do."

"You sound a little off, Ric. Are you okay?"

"Knee's acting up today."

"I'll massage it for you when we get home."

"Thanks."

He and Brooke Drillon were partners. They met at the University of Toronto as undergraduates; Alaric was majoring in electrical and computer engineering, taking advantage of a program that ranked eighth in the world at that time. Brooke was enrolled in criminology and was thinking about a career in law enforcement. They were introduced to each other by mutual friends at a movie night, and it went from there.

Brooke liked to talk to him about her studies. One day, she said that there was no possible way he would do well in her courses. Computer engineering was as safe as houses for him, she insisted, and there wasn't a chance he'd step out of his comfort zone for something he knew nothing about.

He switched programs the next day. To his surprise, he discovered he liked it. When they graduated, he finished seventh in their class. Brooke, of course, was third.

She was immediately recruited by the RCMP as an intelligence analyst. Alaric preferred to apply for a job with the OPP because of its size and the number of different opportunities it presented. Fortunately, he was able to pass the physical and, after completing his courses at the police college, he was posted to Huntsville in the Central region. He started in Traffic like every other stiff but soon showed a knack for picking up information, and he became friends with the regional intelligence officer there. After that, his work had slanted toward the intel side of the playing field

"So," he said, "what can you tell me about Cobalt Strike?"

"The basic structure of the group they're looking at, and a couple of names."

"Fire away, my dear."

"Operationally, it runs out of the Port of Montreal. The gang there is commanded by a Brazilian, Theo Pereira Almeida. About thirty longshoremen work for him as part of the car theft ring. They have several satellite operations in Quebec and Ontario. The closest to you is in Brockville, because it's seen as a good location on the Toronto-to-Montreal corridor. The guy running the show there is Miguel Santos Barbosa, a.k.a. Mike Santos. He owns a container business in Brockville, selling them to residential and commercial customers, so it's a perfect cover. A word of caution: he's under constant surveillance, so stay away."

"Will do."

"There are a bunch of cooling spots scattered around eastern Ontario. The Cobalt guys are still in the process of finding them. They know yours is somewhere in Lanark, but they haven't found it yet. If you could help with that, my boss would be happy. You'd have to give the info, and the credit, to Savard, though."

"That's no problem."

"Glad to hear it. The guy running it is said to be Bruno Ribeiro. A real hard case. He used to have Theo Pereira's job at the port, but things got hot and he was sent out. Took a crew with him from the port. These are the guys you're looking for."

"Thanks, Brooke. Want me to pick up some take-out for tonight?"

"No, I'll get it. I'll probably be home long before you. What do you want?"

"Moroccan?"

"You're so predictable."

They said their goodbyes, and Alaric ended the call. He knew a little more than he had before, but he still hadn't put his hands on the golden ticket.

Sighing, he looked up Gilles Savard's number. The man had never liked him, and now that he was a detective sergeant he would no doubt be even more difficult to deal with. Ah well. The price of admission, he told himself.

CHAPTER 35

Ron Hayward was no hero. After a couple of hours in a cell, enough time for his body to begin metabolizing the alcohol in his bloodstream to the extent that he was able to focus on the situation he was in, he asked for Kevin. Begged and pleaded, really.

"Ron," Kevin said, closing the interview room door behind him, "are you ready to show a little respect now?"

"Yeah, sorry, man. A little too much brew."

"Where'd you get the Merc?"

"That damned little weasel. Should never have fucked around with that guy."

"Who?"

"Millen, goddamn him."

Kevin was surprised. "You mean Gerry Millen let you steal his own motor?"

"No, no, no. Hell's the matter with you? I'm talking about his brother."

"Harry Millen?"

"Yeah, yeah. Guy shows up with it in the back of his van, for chrissakes. Even swiped the wooden stand for it."

"So you bought it off him to flip."

"That's right. Nice piece of equipment." Hayward wiped his mouth on the back of his hand. "I want a deal for giving you that little turd."

"I can't make any promises," Kevin said. "That's all up to the Crown."

"Yeah, yeah, yeah, but you put in a good word for me, man."

"So who do you flip your stuff to, Ron?"

Hayward looked away. "I shouldn't ought to say."

"Why not?"

"Scary dude. Mean as a snake, man."

"I'll need the name."

"And I need to hang onto my health, right?"

"We'll come back to that. Is Flood in on the deal?"

"Walt?" Hayward laughed. "The old dude? Hell, no. Rubber Worm Man. He's completely clueless. Stuff goes on right under his nose like you wouldn't believe."

"So this guy you won't name rents a slip from Flood, comes and goes—from where? Where's he based?"

"I'm not sure, but I think Kingston."

"What makes you say that?"

"He said something one time about having Frontenacs season tickets. Always yapping about hockey."

"Happen to know the registration number on his boat?"

Hayward shook his head. "I don't stick my nose out too far. It's one of them pocket cruisers, I think they call them. Forty-seven foot or something. He calls it the *Flying Vee*."

"Well, hey, Ron. That'll help. But you still won't give me his name?"

"Look, I don't, uh, actually know his name. He told me to call him Sam, so that's what I call him. Sam. Could be his real name is something else, man. Haven't a clue."

"Okay. Different question. Do you fence cars, too?"

Hayward looked shocked. "Shit, no way. That racket's already tied up."

"Who's tying it up?"

"Look, man, I'm, like, trying to help you out as part of our deal, but I don't wanna rat on people like them. I got lots to say about Millen, if you like that tune."

"Okay. Millen. Is he just a freelancer, stealing from his own brother, or does he belong to some gang?"

Hayward snorted. "Lone wolf, man. Nobody would work with a scum bucket like him. Got a nose problem, if you know what I mean." He sniffed loudly.

"So what about Sam? Is he part of a stolen car gang?"

"I doubt it. I think he's got other connections

somewhere else."

"What kind of connections, Ron?"

"Dunno. And what I don't know won't kill me. I'm just a fence, man. I fit here in the middle," he moved the edge of his hand up and down, "and I don't pay too much attention to who's on the left or the right. As long as their cash is good, I'm happy."

"Cash, huh?"

"Yeah. I don't go in for that crypto crap."

"And the car theft guys? Tell me about them."

"I try to stay clear of them dudes. So there's not a lot I can say."

"Give me what you can."

Hayward hesitated. "Head guy's name is Bruno. Mean fucking bastard. In a wheelchair. It's my understanding the bunch of them come from Montreal. The waterfront. Bruno's some kind of stone-cold killer."

Kevin stared at him.

"Christ, man. I'm just a local yokel. I don't know these imports, okay? I heard there's a guy named Junior. Bruno's second-in-command. A slimy little prick they call Squid. Their wheelman. And his sidekick, some nerdy electronics goofball. And a bunch of mechanics and shit."

"They've got a chop shop and cooling spot around here. Where is it?"

"I don't know. Really. Don't know."

"But there is one, right?"

"So I hear." Hayward folded his arms. "That's all I got, pal. Now get me a deal."

CHAPTER 36

Lying on her cot, Ellie continued to think about the girl, Cindy Paige. She wasn't sure why her mind kept turning back to that case, and why it replayed itself in her head each time the drug they gave her started to take hold. Maybe because it was her first homicide investigation as a detective constable. Maybe, as well, because it seemed to trigger a lot of other memories. By association, mostly, and jumbled up across the timeline of her life.

She wondered if Cindy would have become a good basketball player, if she'd lived. Ellie regretted debating the subject with the coach, Mrs. Gordon, that day. She'd sensed Brand's disapproval of her attitude toward the woman, but she'd instantly disliked her and didn't appreciate the way she was demeaning a dead child.

It was not something she would do today, probably. She'd learned the value of professional restraint over the years, not only from Brand's influence on her but also from the model presented by Detective Inspector Carol Duncan, whom she'd admired from afar. She learned how to depersonalize and objectify the things she encountered on the job. How to be calm and observant, like Duncan. How to maintain control and make others believe in your leadership.

Of course, Duncan would never have jumped up on a table to shout down the noise the way Ellie had during the investigation of Constable Maynard's murder. She would never have eaten breakfast in the shower without knowing what she was doing, as Ellie had done during the excavation of a body near Rideau Ferry. She would never have resorted to throwing a bucket of stones into a lake to reduce the stress of another difficult day on the job.

No. Carol Duncan was an elegant swan, and Eleanor March had always been an ugly duckling.

Still. The sedative, or whatever it was, was working its associative voodoo on her once again, and she couldn't help but compare poor Cindy's short-lived attempt at student athleticism with her own, which had been a high point of her youth.

She remembered the day of the Toronto school division championship game in her senior year. Jarvis had dominated all season, finishing in first place with Ellie as the top scorer, third in assists, and sixth in rebounds.

This was Eleanor March at seventeen years of age.

Shortly before it was time for her to leave, her gym

bag packed and ready to go, she went downstairs into the shop to ask Paul if he'd consider attending the game. While she waited for his attention, she watched him serving a customer, a young woman trying to find the right pair of shoes for her wedding.

She was a tall, skinny woman with mouse-brown hair and wide feet. She was very nervous and introverted. She had come alone to the shop so there would be no family or friends looking over her shoulder. The colour of the dress would be white, so Paul confirmed she would want white shoes.

The next hurdle was the height of the heel. She'd never worn high heels before but she had accepted that it would be expected. She was afraid of falling in them or twisting her ankle or breaking off one of the heels at the exact wrong moment.

Ellie watched Paul work through each worry with the same extreme patience he showed with her. Every problem that the woman dwelled on was his problem as well, his to try to solve with her in a comfortable, inexpensive way.

First he measured her feet to get the size, noting the wideness and the fact that her right foot was fractionally larger than her left foot. He spoke to her quietly, without pressure, his Polish accent soft and round, the occasional dropped articles and word endings sounding to Ellie's ear as charming and worthy of affection as ever.

The scar at the corner of his mouth pulled his lip down, his legacy from having been pistol-whipped during the robbery two years ago. It prevented him from smiling, a permanent reminder that life would be something that would test a person every day. His pleasures, however slight, would be experienced without an outward sign of happiness.Once he understood what the woman wanted and what she needed for a comfortable fit, he brought out a selection of white shoes in various styles and with varying height in the heel. He told her just to look at them for a minute while he spoke to his daughter.

Ellie asked him if he would attend her basketball game at the school tonight. He smiled sadly and said, "This is not something we do, Eleanor. We think about you tonight but we do not go to your school events. The way it is."

Ellie watched him turn back to his customer. Was he kinder to her than he was to his own daughter? No, he was kind to everyone. She'd learned not to take his refusals personally. He was an introverted, sad man who'd been traumatized by his experiences at home during the war. That he and Mary had survived to reach Canada and start a new life was almost more than he'd ever hoped for.

She was proud of her accomplishments at school, and she wanted Paul and Mary to be proud of them, too. He praised her for her report cards, which were always exceptional, but never for her athletic accomplishments. She never quite understood why.

She scored 18 points that night, along with 11 assists and 4 rebounds. Jarvis won by 16 points and she came home, dropped off by a friend's parents, a champion. Paul was in the living room, listening to a Polish broadcast on CHIN radio.

"Did you win?"

"Yes."

"This is something. Good night, Eleanor."

It was the last organized basketball game in which she would ever play.

SEPTEMBER 2002

CHAPTER 37

They were floundering. At least that's how Ellie felt. The forensic pathologist had clearly indicated that Cindy Paige had been strangled before falling off the cliff and bashing her head on the rocks below. He believed the blunt force trauma had been the cause of death, that she'd still been alive when she went over the edge, but they didn't know whether she fell or was pushed, which might make the difference between murder and manslaughter.

She was fretting away at random details while Brand walked around muttering to himself. So they did what many detectives often do when staring at a blank wall.

They went to lunch.

Brand drove them down to Guelph and led the way into a tiny hole-in-the-wall Greek restaurant a block from the university campus. He was friends with the owner, a man named Nikos Fotakis, who led them to a table at the back currently occupied by two students who were lingering over dessert. He ran them out, cleared off the table, and seated them without further ado.

Brand ordered baked zucchini fritters for their appetizer and spinach pie for himself. Ellie, on Nikos's recommendation, decided to try the moussaka, a beef-and-eggplant dish that turned out to be absolutely delicious, dripping with olive oil and spiced with cinnamon, oregano, thyme, and chopped tomatoes. It was a bit heavy for lunch, but she was starving and had already developed a reputation for having a cast-iron stomach, able to eat pretty much anything at all. This, though, was a treat.

After the meal, Brand ordered coffee that came in small cups and had the consistency of liquid mud, with foam on the top and grounds at the bottom. Brand added sugar to his but Nikos, who seemed to have taken a shine to Ellie, brought her a small container of honey. She poured a dollop and immediately knew that she'd never drink coffee any other way again.

Eventually the meal was over. Tables had emptied in the tiny restaurant, and they could talk.

"Did you call Ident?"

"Yeah," Ellie said.

"Who'd you talk to?"

"Dearborn."

Brand nodded. There were four identification constables working at the Mount Forest forensic identification facility under the supervision of Identification Sergeant Stan

Beatty. Identification Constable Dean Dearborn specialized in footprints and tire treads. Brand figured he was a solid guy.

Dearborn had worked on tire tread impressions taken from the Paige driveway and the parking area at the hiking trail. At that time, in 2002, he'd relied on visual comparison to attempt to match up different prints. A tire tread identification database wouldn't exist until 2007, and so the work was done on a subjective basis, with different examiners leaning in different directions when it came to significant features, procedures, and methods of capturing prints for analysis. Making three-dimensional moulds using casting material, for example, was often hit-or-miss, and techniques like electrostatic dusting were unreliable. For his part, Dearborn stuck to photography and sketches.

Dearborn was the kind of guy who took his work seriously enough to have started his own personal database. He visited car dealerships and automotive tire stores, photographing and documenting their inventory, and he talked to mechanics and technicians about brand characteristics, wear patterns, and anything else he could think of to ask them. He convinced a colleague to build him a Microsoft Access database to organize his information, and while it was highly unlikely that any of it would stand up as evidence in court, he still felt he was moving in the right direction.

Justin Paige's driveway was paved, and the road itself was perpetually dusty, so he was able to find a number of discrete track marks. One he was able to match right away to Paige's vehicle. Another was a larger tire, which Paige suggested was likely a delivery truck that had stopped a day or so ago with several packages. A few phone calls had confirmed that theory.

"He's got one other from the driveway he hasn't matched yet."

"What about the hiking trail?"

"A dog's breakfast," he said. "There's not much room to park, as you remember, and there'd been enough vehicles in and out to make a hash out of a lot of the prints. He's still working on them."

"What else have we got, Eleanor? What do we know?"

Ellie leaned forward, tapping her fingertip on the table. "More like what we don't know. We know she went from her house to the trail, but we don't know how she got there. Everyone we ask says they didn't give her a ride. She didn't bicycle, because it's still sitting in the garage. So that's Question Number One we still haven't answered."

"Keep going."

"Question Number Two: who would be so upset with her that they'd force her there, run her up a path to a cliff, choke the living daylights out of her, and then watch her fall to her death? That'd take a lot of anger or hatred or something, don't you think?"

"Yeah, I think."

Ellie grabbed a paper placemat from the table across from them and folded it in half to give her a blank page. She fumbled in her jacket pocket and brought out a stub of a pencil. "Who do we know?"

Brand grinned. He waved Nikos over. "Bring me one of those Gazozo things, will you?"

"Gazoza? Orange or lemon?"

"Lemon. Eleanor?"

"Orange. Thanks. Okay." She'd been scribbling down names. "Working from the immediate family outward, right? That's what you've told me. The father and the ex-wife are the only two family members, plus Dawn's boyfriend, Bill Orton. I'd like to interview all of them again, this time at Rockwood. Lean on them a bit."

"Okay."

"School. Mrs. Gordon and Mr. Hamilton. We need a list of the other teachers she had. Friends. Madison, Robert. Madison says she didn't have any enemies. Anyway, it doesn't feel like a kid's crime. How does a kid get her from her house to the cliff? Doesn't make sense."

"No. I agree."

Niko brought their beverages. Brand sipped and smacked his lips.

"Parents of Madison and Robert. They go on the list, but I didn't get any weird vibes from them, and I believed them when they said they didn't give her a ride to the trail. What about you?"

"I agree," he said again, watching her from the corner of his eye.

"Is somebody sitting in the weeds, Leif? Someone I'm forgetting?"

"Let's get the list of her teachers and check them out.

Other than that, we'll have to keep on digging and see what pops."

"Someone who really didn't like this kid," Ellie said.

CHAPTER 38

Ellie watched the video feed in the observation room as Brand went through the preliminaries with Justin Paige. There was some confusion about the attorney caution, and Brand was obligated to assure him he was there of his own free will and could leave at any time.

"I gotta tell you though, Mr. Paige, my questions are gonna be a little different than before. Just as a heads-up to you. We're not playing games here. You need to stay focused and answer all of them with the truth. Understood?"

"Sure," Paige replied uncertainly.

"I want you to tell me first of all what you do for a living. You work at home, is that right?"

"Yes. I'm a day trader."

"What exactly is that, now? Money's kind of a stranger to me, if you know what I mean."

Paige laughed nervously. "I buy and sell stocks and

commodities and sell them before the close of business the same day for a profit. Usually."

"Wow. Okay. Do you pick them out of a hat, or what?"

"No, no. I'm a voracious reader. I check the news every morning, everything I can get access to, in Canada, the US, Hong Kong, all the hotspots that affect the market. I focus on certain commodities, like gold, copper, crude oil, for example. I've done extensive research on them over the past several years until I have a pretty good idea that the price will bump up after I make a quick buy. Coffee I'm good at, but stuff like corn, oats, or wheat I haven't spent enough time with to make any risky trades."

"And, like, stocks, too?"

"Of course. There might be something in the entertainment news, for example, that tells me Paramount Global might get a little bump up during the day. Another example is Nvidia might have recovered from a bad quarterly report, which caused their stock price to drop by almost a third, but I saw where they were making an important acquisition two months ago so I bought in really low, a *Fortune Magazine* profile published the same day, and they shot up enough I was able to make a nice little profit in the same trading session."

"Christ. You must have nerves of steel."

"I drink a lot of coffee."

"One thing, though. I thought that 9/11 blew the crap out of investing. Biggest losses in history, right? How'd you manage to stay afloat over the past year?"

"You'd think it'd be rocky, but I trusted my research and

went with gold, for example, which climbed like crazy over the short term. I shorted travel stocks and entertainment, and bought communications and pharmaceuticals. Here's something interesting I found out later. Did you know that American Airlines and United Airlines stock activity rose big-time immediately before the attack as people shorted them more than twenty-five times the usual volume? So that begs the question. Who knew the attack was coming and took advantage of it?"

"Ever break the law, Mr. Paige? Get in on a little insider trading like that?"

He shook his head emphatically. "I'm a low-risk, low-reward kind of guy. I'll take a half dozen small profits over the course of a day and that's it. Insider trading is the kind of high-risk bullshit that'll kill a career every time."

"Nobody holding something over your head? Using your daughter as leverage?"

"No! What a terrible thing to say!"

"Might be a good time to talk to me about it. We might be able to help you out."

"Jesus! There's nothing like that. Why would you even think there would be?"

"Keep your focus, Mr. Paige. Like I said, we're going to go around the merry-go-round a few times on stuff."

Watching from the video room, Ellie thought Brand was doing a good job applying pressure. He'd started off mildly enough, with what seemed like genuine curiosity about how Paige made his money, then had suddenly turned on the heat. Now he was going to shift gears, and she thought she knew where he was going next.

"We're trying to figure out how Cindy got to the hiking trail from your house. Did you give her a ride down there?"

"No, of course not. I've told you what happened."

"Did she get on your nerves, Mr. Paige? Teenagers can be like that. Drive you nuts. Did it get too much after a while?"

"No, of course not. She was everything to me."

"Did you take her down to the trail, have an argument, chase her to the cliff and push her over?"

"No, no. You've got it all wrong."

"Let's say for a minute you didn't take her down there. Who would have?"

"I don't know."

"Did you hear a car in the driveway when you were out in the garden?"

"No. Like I told you, I had my earbuds in. Listening to BBC News."

"Actually, Mr. Paige, you didn't tell us that. I'd have remembered."

"Well, that's what happened. I couldn't hear anything."

"Someone obviously came in and got her, whether you heard them or not. Who would it have been?"

"I don't *know*."

"Did she often go out like this without telling you?"

"No, never. I always told her, 'Let me know if you're going out.' We live in a rural area, and I need to know."

"When she went hiking, what did she take with her?"

"Her backpack."

"What would she take in the backpack?"

"Water; energy bars; extra pair of socks; a small first aid kit. I always checked before she left."

"And she didn't take the backpack with her this time, did she?"

He shook his head.

"Did you have a fight with her? Maybe a disagreement at the breakfast table?"

"I've already told you, no. She was sleeping when I had my breakfast. Then I went out in the garden. You're asking me these questions because you think I had something to do with her disappearance. Do you know how absurd that is?"

"She enjoyed hiking, I take it."

"Yes, she liked to be physically active."

"Did you go with her?"

"Only at first. Then she started going with friends at school. They'd come to pick her up with their mother and bring her back home afterwards."

"Anyone in particular?"

"Oh, there was mostly a group of four. Give me a minute. A boy, uh, Marc Rule. I don't know his parents. And two girls. Brandy, no Brittany Stevens, and the other one, uh, Kim something. I can't remember her last name. It was usually Mrs. Stevens driving them in a passenger van. She's some kind of artist. Watercolourist, I think. She'd paint while she was waiting for them to finish their hike."

More names for the list, Ellie thought, jotting them down.

"How was she making out with the move to high school?"

"A little rough for her at first. You know how it is. In Grade Eight you're at the top of the ladder, and suddenly you change schools for Grade Nine and you're back down at the bottom of the pile again. One of a thousand different new kids."

He seemed to have calmed down a little, Ellie thought.

"Was it important for her to be important? Popular?"

"No, it's not that. It's just a matter of self-confidence and self-esteem. It's like the entire school suddenly treats you as completely insignificant."

Suddenly, the man began to cry. End of interview.

CHAPTER 39

The next morning Bill Orton occupied the hot seat, with Brand presiding once again. Waiting in the on-deck circle was Dawn Paige, who would be Ellie's quarry. Dawn wasn't scheduled to work until four o'clock in the afternoon, but Orton had been forced to take leave from his job, so he was a little pissed off to have been driven up to Rockwood from Guelph. No one sympathized with him.

Brand walked in with a can of Coke and a plastic cup. He opened the Coke and filled the cup, giving it to Orton. After the preliminaries, Brand questioned Orton on his background.

"You're a Guelph boy, are you?"

"Uh huh."

"Education?"

"Quit school after Grade Eleven."

"How long have you worked at Old Dutch?"

"Since I quit school."

"Have you had any other jobs?"

"Nah. It's a good job."

"What about your parents?"

"Both dead."

"Other family?"

"Two brothers."

"Where are they?"

"I don't know. We don't keep in touch." He drank some Coke and belched softly.

"How well did you know Cindy Paige?"

"Not real well. She was Dawny's problem, not mine."

"Did she come around to visit?"

"Oof, only a couple of times. They fought like cats and dogs. The kid was real surly."

"She was a cute thing, though, eh?"

"Yeah."

"Did she like your truck?"

Orton frowned at him. "My truck?"

"You gave her rides now and then, didn't you?"

"Nope. That never happened."

"Make a move on her?"

"You're off base, man. Not my type. I don't go for kids."

He was a handsome goofball, Ellie conceded. Dark wavy hair; pouty Elvis lips; broad shoulders; tall. Younger than Dawn Paige by several years. Probably attracted to her obvious physical charms.

"Somebody gave her a ride to that hiking trail last Saturday. Who do you think that was?"

"I don't know; I was at work."

"No theories to share with me?"

"Theories?" he snorted. "I don't get into that shit."

"What about Dawn? Do you think maybe she gave Cindy a ride?"

"I don't know, I said. I was at work. But I doubt it. They really didn't like each other. I'm not sure how many times I have to say that."

"How long have you and Dawn known each other?"

"Uh, a while."

"Did you know her while she was still married to Paige?"

He shrugged. "I guess so."

"Where'd you meet?"

"In a bar, in Guelph. That's where people usually hook up, isn't it?"

"Which bar?"

"The Wickshire, on Wyndham."

Ellie knew the place by reputation. It was a cocktail bar that didn't cater to students. It was a popular spot for older women, divorced or looking to be. It was informally known as The Cougar Inn.

"I liked to stop in there first to check out that crowd before trying the crazier places," Orton was saying. "I'm not into the younger kids, like I said. Older women have their act together and they know what they want. I like that."

"So that's where you met Dawn?"

Orton nodded.

"You knew she was married?"

"Sure, she was up front about it. Hadn't stopped me before. There's a kind of, uh, desperation about married women. That's why they go there. The sex can be pretty wild."

"What did she tell you about herself? Where's she from?"

He shrugged. "Out west somewhere. I think she said Winnipeg. Or maybe Regina. I'm not sure."

"Did she say what she did before she came east?"

"Nah, she never talks about that. My guess is she must have been an exotic dancer or something. With that build."

"Why would she marry a guy like Justin Paige?"

Orton made a noise. "Dunno. No idea. Money, I guess."

"And him? Why would he marry someone like her?"

"Are you kidding? He had to be looking at the same stuff I've been looking at. Wowsa."

"What were your impressions of Justin?"

"Her ex? Shit, I dunno. Okay guy, I guess. A bit of a dweeb. Newshound. Not much fun to be around. Why?"

"Just asking questions, Bill. How often were you up to his place?"

"Me? Never. Why stir up trouble? I swiped his wife from him, so I severely doubt he'd be interested in having a beer with me on the front porch."

"So you didn't have anything to do with him?"

"That's what I'm saying. Zip. Nada. I steered clear of the dude."

The interview wound up and Orton left. Brand emptied the plastic cup into the wastepaper basket and bagged it as evidence.

CHAPTER 40

Ellie walked into the interview room with a bottle of water and a plastic cup. She opened the water, filled the cup, and gave it to Dawn Paige, who ignored it.

After covering the preliminaries, including a reminder that Dawn was here of her own free will and could leave at any time, as well as pointing out that the interview was being recorded, Ellie had decided to follow Brand's lead with Orton by asking basic questions about her past to get a sense of her willingness to talk.

Ellie was fresh from her detective training program at the police college, which had included advanced courses on interviewing and interrogation, and she was aware that Brand's approach was similar to the famous technique developed by John Reid back in the day. Reid was a former Chicago cop and polygraph examiner whose work with Fred Inbau, a criminologist who was the director of the Chicago crime lab, had mixed results in practice, as it tended to produce its share of false confessions, particularly among younger people. Most interrogators in Canada used a modified version when it seemed appropriate to do so, including Brand.

Being something of a non-conformist at heart, Ellie was exploring her own approach to advanced questioning, relying on patience, basic listening skills, and good instincts. She intended to develop her own technique to as high a level as she possibly could.

"Where did you meet Justin Paige, Dawn?"

"In the Wickshire."

"The cocktail lounge."

"Mmm hmm."

"Wait, isn't that where you met Bill Orton?"

"I guess so."

"Did you go there often?"

"Not really. I worked nearby, at City Hall, and sometimes I'd grab a drink after my shift before taking the bus home."

"City hall? What did you do there?"

"Custodial. My shift was after hours, four to nine. I emptied wastepaper baskets, cleaned toilets, swept the floors, and that kind of crap."

"Is that what you do now, at the university?"

"SSDD, dear. Same shit, different day."

"Where are you from, originally?"

"Around."

Ellie decided to bare her teeth a little. "Let me explain

something to you. The forensic pathologist has ruled that the manner of Cindy's death is undetermined. Which means the coroner wants us to continue our investigation to find out whether she died accidentally or was pushed over that cliff by someone. Understand?"

"Sure."

"Fine, then answer my questions when I ask them. Where were you born and raised?"

Dawn studied the ceiling as though summoning enough patience to respond. "Winnipeg."

"What's your date of birth?"

"April 19."

"Year?"

"1966. That's what I was told, anyway."

"Who were your parents?"

"I don't know. I grew up in an orphanage."

"Which one?"

"Johnson Home."

"What about school?"

"What about it? I got out as soon as these started getting too much attention from the teachers." She cupped her breasts. "Same thing at the orphanage. It was safer to be out on my own."

"What did you do?"

"Went to work. Doing whatever they'd pay me to do. I washed dishes, swept floors, cleaned hotel rooms, whatever I could get. I always told them I was eighteen, and I looked like twenty-two. Then I got married."

"Oh? Who'd you marry?"

"A guy named Bob Watson. He was a bouncer and bartender at a bar. A lot older than me. He got me a job waiting on tables. Good tips."

"How long were you and Watson married?"

"Three long years. Then he got shot robbing a convenience store and I divorced him while he was in prison. Now you're getting the whole story, eh, lady? The whole pity party."

"What did you do then?"

"I got the hell out of the Peg, that's what I did. Went to Brandon. I was nineteen. I felt like I was thirty."

"So this was in 1985?"

"I don't know. I guess so. Who keeps track of the date when you're living hand to mouth all the time and dodging the pimps and pick-up artists?"

"How long were you in Brandon?"

"A while. I hooked up with a guy who treated me decent, and I settled in for a couple of years, I guess it was."

"What was the guy's name?"

"Aldress. Terry Aldress."

"So tell me about him."

"What do you want me to say?"

"Whatever," Ellie said carelessly. "What did he do? What was he like?"

She made a face. "He was pretty weird. Not bad looking, but very fucked up. He managed a physiotherapy place downtown but it was actually a massage parlour with an escort service out the back door. He had a lot of money. At first he wanted me to be one of the girls, but I said no."

"Did he give you money?"

"Sometimes, but I had a job. I worked in a pet store."

"How long were you with him?"

"Shit, about four years, I guess. Then one night I said no and he raped me, so I packed up and took off. Ended up coming to Ontario with a guy who was driving to Guelph to take a job at the university as a groundskeeper. He was a creep too, so I didn't hang around him long."

"What was *his* name?"

"Christ, I don't know. Walter. Something. Can't remember now. Flushed him down the toilet like a bad crap."

So you came to Ontario in 1998?"

"I guess so."

"And that same year, in 1998, you married Justin Paige?"

"Sounds about right."

"How old was Cindy then?"

"I don't know. A kid."

"And you didn't get along."

Dawn snorted. "She hated me, right off. I wasn't supposed to replace her dead mom. She was a little sniper. Always snipe, snipe, sniping at me. Little bitch."

"Was it just arguing? Or did you get physical with her?"

Dawn didn't answer right away. Ellie waited.

"Yeah, I gave her a slap in the mouth one time. I caught her stealing my stuff. Some costume jewelry and bottles of perfume. She was selling them to kids at school. I gave her shit and she gave me lip right back, so I lost it and gave her one right across her nasty mouth."

"What happened?"

"She went crying to daddy and I got blasted for it." She shook her head. "*That* was the beginning of the end, as far as I was concerned."

"Just a slap? Or were you rougher than that with her? Maybe you gave her a good shaking, or hit her with something?"

"Nah. Just that one slap. Although I must admit there was a pretty good windup behind it."

"You hated her, didn't you?"

"No, no. I sure as hell didn't like her, but hate's too strong a word."

"Tell me again where you were on Saturday morning when Cindy disappeared."

"I was in the city. I went shopping. Like I told you before."

"We checked, and no one remembers you being there. You've got to do better than this, Dawn."

"No, I don't. Burden of proof's on you, young lady, not me."

"Maybe you didn't go shopping. Maybe you went to Justin's place, argued with Cindy, put her in your car, took her out to the boonies and killed her."

"You're full of shit."

"Am I? We blew up your alibi, Dawn. You can't account for your whereabouts."

"I was nowhere near that little bitch."

"I think you were. Why don't you tell me about it. You hated her."

"I just said I didn't."

"But you did, didn't you? You hated her."

"*I didn't hate her!*" Dawn slapped her hands down on the table. "Get it through your fucking head, damn it! I didn't do anything to her!"

Gotcha.

"All right, Dawn. That's all for now. You can go."

As soon as she was alone in the room, Ellie looked at the camera and told Brand to send for a scenes-of-crime officer to collect Dawn's handprints from the table.

The life story she'd given her might have been true, or it might have been total bullshit. The fact that she'd suddenly loosened her tongue and started in with the autobiographical sketch had seemed a little off-base.

Maybe her prints would tell them a different story.

CHAPTER 41

It was a Saturday, but here they were back at Fergus District High School, pounding on the oak double front doors trying to attract the attention of someone who could let them in.

"Let's try around the back," Ellie suggested, the edge of her fist getting sore from pounding.

"Here's someone," Brand said.

A middle-aged man came down the stairs and wandered toward them.

Brand pounded. The man shrugged. Brand held up his badge and warrant card.

The man shrugged again and shuffled forward, reluctantly opening the door a crack. "School's closed, officer."

"There's a drama club here this morning. They're using the auditorium."

"Oh, them. Sure." He opened the door wide enough for Brand to grab its edge before turning away. "The back door's open for them. You can leave that way, if you like."

"Great. Which way to the auditorium?"

"Follow me. I'll show you."

The auditorium had two doors, one at each end. The man opened the closest one and, with a grand gesture, waved him inside. He closed the door after them, and they never saw him again.

The house lights were off in the back half of the seating area, so they walked down the aisle from darkness into light. People were scattered around in the first few rows, mostly adults, and teenagers milling about on the stage, which was configured in a typical proscenium arch layout Ellie recognized from her own school days. A young man seemed to be trying to herd them into position.

One or two spectators glanced at them indifferently as they reached the stage apron, but most of them were focused on the kids, watching with the complete absorption of doting parents.

The young man came over to them. "May I help you with something?"

Brand held up his badge again. "Detective Constable Brand, OPP. This is Detective Constable March. Are you in charge here?"

"I'm the director, so I guess that makes me in charge. Sometimes I wonder." He crouched down, offering his hand. "Peter Glass."

"Mr. Glass, we're looking to talk to three kids we

understand are here. Marc Rule, Brittany Stevens, and, uh, Kim Something."

"They're here, yes. May I ask what this is about?"

"Do you have a minute? Is there somewhere we can talk?"

"Just a sec, okay?"

He stood up and surveyed the stage. Apparently he saw what he wanted. "Do a walk-through of scene two, will you? Morgan? Donald?"

As the teenagers took their places, Glass disappeared into the nearest of the wings. They heard his sneakers thumping down a short set of stairs. He pushed aside a curtain and they joined him in the corner.

"This isn't a school drama club, is it?" Ellie asked.

Glass shook his head. "We're funded by the town. We're an extension of the Central Wellington Drama Club. They give classes to school children from Grade Four to Grade Eight. We offer something for a few exceptional kids who want to continue on with drama after they graduate into high school."

"Why aren't you using the theatre in town?"

"Can't afford it. They charge rent even for something as innocuous as this. The school, on the other hand, lets us come in every Saturday morning for free."

"I see."

"Plus, most of these kids are students here, so we've agreed to give an assembly performance before Christmas. We should be ready by then."

"What are you doing?" Brand asked.

"*Romeo and Juliet.* A very demanding work for high school students, but these kids are here because they should be able to handle it."

"Was Cindy Paige one of your students?" Ellie asked.

"Who? Oh, okay. The girl who was killed. No, she wasn't."

"Where can we talk to the kids?"

Glass thought for a moment. "There's a back door that leads out into the parking lot. Would you be able to take them out there so they won't be centred out? There's a bench out there."

"Are their parents here?"

Glass took a moment to survey the seats before shaking his head. "Only Mrs. Stevens. I think she picks everyone up and drives them."

Brand grunted. "That's her, halfway up, isn't it? With the sketchbook?"

"Uh, yeah."

Brand looked at Ellie. Ellie said, "Together or separate?"

"What do you think?"

"We could do them together, with Mrs. Stevens. Then separate follow-ups, if we need to."

He smiled humorlessly at her. "Would you mind?"

Ellie walked up the stairs until she reached the row where Mrs. Stevens sat, in the approximate middle, just inside the shadow of the unlighted area. She edged over and sat down a couple of seats away, staying clear of the purse and artist's portfolio piled next to her.

"Mrs. Stevens?"

The woman continued stroking the page with her charcoal stick for a moment before glancing up. "Yes?"

Ellie badged her and identified herself. "Detective Constable Brand and I have a few questions for Brittany and a couple of her friends. We need you to sit in on the interview, if you would."

"Friends? You mean Marc and Kim?"

"That's right."

After much sighing and putting away of stuff and smoothing out of skirts and shoving of feet back into sandals, Mrs. Stevens followed Ellie down to where Brand waited for them. Glass was already back on stage with his two leads, Donald as Romeo and Morgan as Juliet.

"We'll have a small platform here," he was saying, "to represent the balcony. Only a couple meters high, so don't worry. It'll be safe. Donald, you'll enter from stage left and deliver your first line—"

"'He jests at scars,'" the boy quoted, "'that never felt a wound.'"

"Correct! At which point a spot will come on from behind you, Morgan, and you'll step into it, looking thoughtfully up at the heavens. Donald, you'll continue with the speech—"

"'But, soft! What light through yonder window breaks! It is the east, and Juliet is the sun!'"

"Sounds like you've got it." He glanced into the wings and saw Brand and Ellie walking through with Mrs. Stevens toward the back. "Okay. Let's run through it."

With Mrs. Stevens' help, they located the three teenagers and herded them out back. A wooden park bench waited for them, as Glass had promised, and several lawn chairs. Brand set up a chair for Mrs. Stevens and got the kids lined up on the bench.

Ellie was up to bat. "Names, please."

"Marc Rule." He was a slender, handsome boy with upswept dark hair, thick eyebrows, and perfect teeth. He made eye contact with Ellie and held it.

"I'm Brittany Stevens. That's my mom." Brittany wore her light brown hair long, down her shoulders in front. Her forehead was a little high and her mouth a bit wide, but her complexion was clear and she radiated the same kind of self-confidence as Marc.

Mrs. Stevens, for her part, was an older version of her daughter—same hair, same facial structure, same demeanour. She'd already whipped out her sketchbook to do her thing.

"Kim Bedford." Here, Ellie thought, was the follower. The girl whose name you had trouble remembering. The girl whose clothing wasn't quite as nice as her friend's. Who wasn't as pretty as her friend. The girl with acne. The girl who avoided eye contact, whose chin was down, whose fingers clutched at the pleats of her skirt.

"Detective Constable Brand and I are here to ask you some questions about Cindy Paige."

None of the three showed any particular reaction to the statement, which Ellie found interesting in itself. They must have been expecting an interview to happen at some point or other in the near future. And now here it was.

"We understand the four of you had some kind of a hiking club?" Ellie waited to see which one would speak first. Which one was the alpha?

"Not exactly a club," Marc said, glancing at Brittany. "Just a group of us."

"We all like hiking," Brittany agreed.

Letting Marc know he'd given a good answer, Ellie saw. Brittany was the alpha.

"How long have you been hiking together?"

"Since Grade Seven," Brittany replied. "We went on a class trip—you know, from Stephen G. McQueen—and it was so much fun we decided to get geared up and make a hobby out of it."

"Christmas gifts," Mrs. Stevens murmured. "Birthday gifts. A long shopping list."

"I know, mom," Brittany grinned, "but at least it's something healthy."

"For a good cause," Mrs. Stevens agreed.

"Did Cindy always go with you, or was it mostly just you three?"

"She was part of the group," Marc said. "We were the Three Musketeers, and Kim was our D'Artagnan."

"Our young Gascon," Brittany laughed.

Marc gave her a nudge and pointed with his chin. Kim had begun to cry, so silently that it had gone unnoticed up to now.

"Buck up," Brittany said to her. "Don't let the team down, now."

"I can't help it," Kim murmured.

Ellie was about to ask what was wrong, but she held her tongue. She wanted to see this play out among the friends. There was something these kids were sitting on.

"Yes, you can," Marc said.

"It's your fault," Kim whispered.

"It's *not* his fault," Brittany said.

"Colin's *his* cousin."

"He was *your* boyfriend," Marc retorted.

"Who's Colin?" Ellie asked.

Silence. The three of them stared at their feet, their hands clasped tightly together. None of them wanted to answer the question.

"Marc?" Mrs. Stevens prompted.

He regarded her bitterly before drawing a long breath. "He's my cousin."

"What's his full name?"

"Colin Rule."

"Why are you suddenly talking about him?"

Silence.

"I wonder," Ellie said to Brand, "if we should take them all to Rockwood and continue this under more formal conditions."

"Maybe. It might remind everyone of the seriousness of the situation."

"Is that necessary?" asked Mrs. Stevens, her charcoal stick still working.

"What do you think, Brittany?" Ellie stared at the alpha. "Do we need to do this formally? In an interview room? With audio and video recording?"

"No."

"So one of you talk to me about Colin."

"He was my boyfriend," Kim said. "Last year. He was in Grade Ten and now he's a Grade Eleven. He's sixteen, and he has a car."

"He's not your boyfriend now?"

"No. When my parents found out how old he was, they made me break up with him."

"I see. Did he go hiking with you?"

"No. He thought it was stupid."

This time, Ellie had bought a few packages of tissues at the store on the way to work this morning, so she took one out of her pocket now and gave it to Kim. Then she looked at Marc.

"This cousin of yours. Did he know Cindy?"

They listened to the rattling of cellophane for a moment as Kim removed a tissue from the package and dabbed at her eyes.

"Yeah." Marc studied the knuckles on his right hand.

"And?"

"He tried to date her."

"And?"

"She wouldn't give him the time of day. She liked Rob Starr."

"And?"

"And," Brittany said, clearly angry now, "he shows up at the hiking trail in his wonderful car and forces Cindy to go off with him."

"Forces her?"

"Colin's a creep, okay? No, I'm sorry Marc, but it's true. He had her by the wrist and threw her into the car and slammed the door on her. You didn't do a damned thing."

"It happened too fast," Marc said. "I didn't know what he was going to do."

"It *didn't* happen too fast. You just stood there and watched."

Ellie could sense that friendships were about to unravel in front of her. "When did this happen?"

"About a month ago. Before school started."

"What did Cindy say about it afterward?"

"She didn't want to talk about it," Brittany said, "but I made her. She said he took her off to the Lookout and made her neck with him."

"The Lookout?"

"Elora Gorge. It's not far, but that's not the point. He *forced* her to go with him. He *forced* her to neck. Isn't that against the law or something?"

"You're making too big a deal out of it," Marc said.

"I am *not*. She was really upset afterward."

"Did she tell anyone about it?" Ellie asked. "Her father?"

"No. She didn't even tell her best pal Madison about it. She only told me because I made her."

"Did he injure her?"

"She had pretty bad bruises on her wrist."

"He just had a crush on her," Marc said. "He wanted her to like him back."

"Sure," Kim whispered, "like he had a crush on me."

"Was he rough with you, too?" Ellie asked.

"Sometimes," Kim said, "a little bit. I was kind of relieved when Dad said I had to break it off. It wasn't very fun."

"Did he force you to have sex?"

Kim looked down, blushing furiously. She shook her head.

"Did he force Cindy to have sex?" Ellie asked Brittany.

"No. She said he didn't go that far."

"So where does Colin Rule live?"

"Next door to me," Marc said.

Ellie looked at him.

"We live in a duplex on St. Charles Street. His dad is my Uncle Charlie. He and my dad are brothers."

Ellie was still learning the landscape within their area of jurisdiction, but she knew that St. Charles Street was situated in a somewhat poorer area of Fergus, near the downtown. Perhaps that explained why Brittany's mother did all the driving. Could be that the other parents couldn't care less about what their kids did outside of school, or were always too busy trying to make ends meet to have the time for them.

In this setting, among a group of privileged children giving up their Saturday mornings for a chance to pursue a dream not shared by many others their age, the three of them had seemed at first to blend right in. But up close, under pressure, they became individuals, youths from different backgrounds, different levels of opportunity, and different odds of grabbing the brass ring.

"What's the address on St. Charles?" Brand asked.

Eyes down, Marc told him.

CHAPTER 42

The duplex on St. Charles Street was a bit run down, Ellie saw, as they pulled up to the curb out front. It was a wide, two-storey frame structure with a long verandah and two entrances, one at each end. The clapboards had faded to some kind of beige-pink hue, weather-worn in spots where the grey wood showed through.

When she'd called in their destination to dispatch and requested a cruiser to meet them there, someone had kindly looked up the address and called Brand with a little background.

"Apparently," he said, shutting off the engine and pulling the keys, "this was once a boarding house for men working at the Beatty factory."

"Beatty?"

"Yeah. Made washing machines and stuff like that. A

big deal in town for quite a while. Then they sold out to GSW in the sixties and only made water heaters after that. This place was sold and converted into the lovely two-family home you see before you now."

"Did he say how long the Rules have been here?"

"The place is owned by a couple of lawyers in Guelph. Bought it as an investment, no doubt."

Ellie snorted.

"Tom Rule, the older brother, has rented 502 for the past sixteen years. His brother Charlie moved in next door two years later. Tom has a record for break and enter, and Charlie is a brawler who gets arrested in bars and brings us out here now and again on domestic call outs."

Ellie looked over her shoulder as one of their cruisers pulled up behind them. Brand glanced in the rear-view mirror and unbuckled. Ellie followed suit.

As Brand and the two uniformed officers conferred, Ellie studied the street. The duplex was on the north side. Beside it on the left was an empty lot with miscellaneous litter caught up in the weeds and overgrown grass. On the right was an equally dilapidated storey-and-a-half house with a patchwork shingle roof and a filthy green front door.

Down the street, past the vacant lot, was a small convenience store, another storey-and-a-half, and a cross-street, Patterson Avenue. Across the road from the duplex, on the south side, were another run-down duplex, an old stone home that had not done well over the passage of time, and a few other small frame houses.

"Knock and talk," Brand said, the two constables stepping up behind him.

Ellie nodded her understanding that she was the one who would do the knocking and talking. This was a standard technique used by law enforcement to enter a residence when they didn't have a warrant, relying on their social engineering skills to obtain consent from the resident to come in, look around, and ask questions.

Ellie approached the right-hand door with caution. The verandah was half-rotted and rickety, and she didn't want to end up putting her foot through a board while trying to make an arrest. The left-hand door opened, and a man stepped out. This was likely Tom Rule, Marc's father. Pressed blue golf shirt; khaki shorts, sandals. Hair combed; clean-shaven.

"What the hell's he done now? Is it Peg again?"

"Please go back inside," Brand said, advancing on him with his hand up, palm forward.

Ellie banged on the door with the edge of her fist. Nothing. She banged again and waited.

The curtain moved sideways and an eye stared out at her.

Ellie showed her badge. "OPP. May we come in?"

The curtain fell back. A chain lock rattled. The door opened a crack.

"What do you want?"

"Are you Mrs. Rule? Margaret Rule? I'm Detective Constable Eleanor March. May we come in?"

"What do you want?"

"We're looking for your son, Mrs. Rule. Colin. Is he here?"

"Why do you want to know?"

Ellie felt Brand right behind her, sensing trouble. "We need to ask him a few questions," she said. "Important questions. You'll be with him the whole time."

"I don't know. What's he done?"

"Please let us in, Mrs. Rule."

As the woman opened the door a bit wider, Ellie had a clear line of sight down the hallway and through the kitchen to a back door. She saw a teenaged boy rush through the kitchen and out the door, disappearing to the left.

"Runner!" Ellie bolted down the length of the verandah as Brand forced the door open and moved Mrs. Rule aside. Ellie felt a board give way beneath her heel but she kept going, off the end of the verandah and around a car parked in the driveway at the side of the house. She saw the youth, presumably Colin Rule, as he ran across the vacant lot.

She set off after him, aware of one of the constables behind her, trying to keep up. Rule cut behind the convenience store and Ellie followed, running at top speed, closing the gap between them.

"Stop! Police!"

The boy looked over his shoulder, stumbled, and headed through a gap between two houses for Patterson Avenue.

As she reached the gap, Ellie briefly considered whether or not she should draw her sidearm. The boy had shown no sign of a weapon, so she left it in her holster.

She emerged onto Patterson and saw the boy a few doors down, still running. She cranked it up, not yet winded, and caught him just before the next intersection. He veered onto someone's front lawn as she grabbed his shoulder and pulled him down. She fell, scrambled to her knees, and cuffed him.

Back at the duplex, warnings and rights administered, Ellie handed him off to the constable, who was still labouring a bit from the chase. Two more cruisers arrived, along with EMS and other vehicles.

Brand shook his head at her. "You're not even breathing hard."

Mrs. Rule came out of the house with the constable who'd followed Brand inside. She got into the back seat of the cruiser behind Brand's car, weeping.

"It's filled with stolen property," Brand said. "Go in and take a look. Looks like they were moving all kinds of stuff out of here. Electronics, clothing, booze, power tools."

"Holy crap."

CHAPTER 43

It was Ellie's arrest, so it was her interrogation.

Although the *Youth Criminal Justice Act* would not come into force until the following April, the current *Young Offenders Act* already provided rights to youths between the ages of twelve and eighteen, including the right to counsel and the right to have a parent or other adult present during questioning.

Colin Rule and his mother spoke to an attorney with Legal Aid, after which they were taken to an interview room. Ellie covered the preliminaries as carefully as she could, conscious of the need for an interrogation that would provide solid results which would hold up in court. Once that ground was covered, she began.

"Colin, how well did you know Cindy Paige?"

"Pretty well, I guess."

"Was she your girlfriend?"

"Yeah, sort of."

"What about Robert Starr? I thought she liked him."

"Nah. I don't think so."

Right away, Ellie could see that he was going to play fast and loose with the truth. "Did you guys date?"

"Yeah, once or twice."

"What did you do on these dates?"

"Went to a movie. Drove down to the Lookout to check out the view."

"When was the last time you took her down there?"

"I don't know. A month ago, I guess."

"Where'd you pick her up?"

Colin hesitated, sensing trouble. "She was hiking with her friends."

"You got rough with her, didn't you?"

"No, I didn't. She was embarrassed about leaving her friends, but she changed her mind. You've been talking to that know-it-all blabbermouth Brittany, haven't you?"

"Where were you last Saturday, Colin?"

"Last Saturday?" Puzzled, he looked at his mother. "We went down to see Gran."

"Colin takes me down every Saturday. We have lunch with her and then we come back in the middle of the afternoon. When she falls asleep."

"Who?"

"My mother," Mrs. Rule said. "She's in long-term care in Guelph. She's eighty-six. Colin drives me down."

"You drive her down to Guelph?" Ellie stared at him.

"Yeah. We have to sign in and out. It's a pain."

"This is where you were last Saturday?"

"Yeah."

"I think you two have cooked up this story between you to cover the fact that you picked up Cindy at her house on Saturday, just before lunch. You drove her to the hiking trail, fought with her, tried to strangle her, and then threw her off a cliff. Isn't that the truth, Colin?"

"No. Where'd you get an idea like that? Brittany?"

"When we process the tire track marks at the parking area down at the trail, we're going to find a match to the tires on your car, aren't we?"

"No."

"Colin's telling the truth," Mrs. Rule said. "And like he told you, we have to sign in at the home and write down the time. And the same when we leave. Ask to see their register. The proof will be there that Colin's telling the truth, that he was with me when this girl died."

"Why did you run when I came to the door?"

He stared at her. "You're kidding, right?"

"No, I'm not kidding. Why did you run?"

"Did you see the stuff in our house?"

"I saw it."

"Then you know why I got the hell out of there."

Ellie stood up. "Wait here. Another detective wants to ask you some other questions. About all that stuff in your house you were scared we'd see."

"With a warrant?" Mrs. Rule calmly asked.

"You bet your pretty pink socks, ma'am. A bunch of them. Don't go anywhere."

PRESENT DAY

PRESENT DAY

The woman had just taken Ellie for a bathroom break. Back in the room, Ellie sat down on the cot as Junior came in. As the woman walked past him on her way out, Junior gave her bottom a pat and a squeeze. The woman threw him a look that Ellie thought was mostly impish as she closed the door behind her.

"Is that your wife?"

Junior grinned. "Her? Nah. Just a friend."

Ellie lay down and put her head on the pillow. "What would your wife say about you flirting with your friends?"

"What she don't know don't hurt her. Drink this."

Ellie turned her face to avoid the straw he was pushing at her. "Enough drugs."

"Hey, drink. This stuff is the only thing between you

and a bullet in the forehead right now. Don't give Bruno an excuse, okay?"

Ellie drank.

He left without her noticing it. The room was cold and the blanket they'd given her was thin, and she shivered until her awareness of each passing moment began to dim. Cold, hot. What the hell. Would she ever reach a tolerance level with this stuff where it would stop working and she could maintain her grip on reality long enough to do something about her predicament?

Her thoughts drifted. Junior wasn't stupid, just over-confident. The last thing she would do is develop a Stockholm Syndrome thing with them, Junior in particular, because they were criminals and she was a cop. Of course, there had been a few crooks she'd almost become fond of, in a law enforcement way. The 'Ndrangheta guys in Vaughan, for example. And Junior was friendly, which was helping her get through this ordeal.

And yet, at the end of the day, he was a creep as well as a criminal. She disliked infidelity and always had. Playing fast and loose with a woman other than his wife crossed another line, as far as she was concerned.

It was because of Gareth, of course.

So many bad memories. So many failures. She blamed herself for his inability to remain faithful to her. She'd kept her own name, rather than become Eleanor Miller. Mrs. Gareth Miller. The faceless, nameless one. She'd focused on her own career instead of on him and *his* career and *his* interests and *his* priorities.

She'd asked him once, when they both had had a little too much to drink, why he'd married her.

"I thought it'd be amusing to date a cop. Then you told me you were pregnant and I thought I'd better do the right thing."

How charming. How romantic.

This was Eleanor March at twenty-six years of age.

Melanie was a year old. Gareth was celebrating his thirty-first birthday. That's why they'd been drinking, she remembered now. They'd gone out to dinner with a group of his friends, Gareth showing off a new grey Hugo Boss suit with a black tie, his Cary Grant look, and Ellie uncomfortable in a black skirt suit and blue blouse.

An economics professor at York University, Gareth was beginning to work his way up the ladder as an apparatchik of the federal Progressive Conservative Party, and the people celebrating with them were mostly fellow PCs. Joe Clark was still leading the party, but those around the table, Gareth especially, believed that their future lay in a merger with the Reform Party-slash-Canadian Alliance, despite Clark's fierce opposition to any sort of unification process.

Preston Manning had lost the leadership of the Alliance to Stockwell Day, and while Gareth was disdainful of Day's wackadoodle creationism beliefs and his adherence to Christian Right policies, they all knew that Clark's days were numbered, Red Toryism having run its course, and that Stephen Harper was looming on the horizon. The numbers showed that Chrétien was about to win a third term, and change was inevitable.

Once they put Day's dinosaur nonsense behind them and morphed back into legitimacy as a united party with a leader like Harper at their head, their economic policies would regain their proper place as a central plank in the new right-wing platform that would carry them into power. Which was where Gareth came in. He was determined to ride the wave to greater heights as their go-to economics guru.

It was a horrible dinner for Ellie. She was treated as a novelty by a few of the guests and then quickly forgotten as politics dominated the table talk for the rest of the evening. Gareth ignored her, his eyes bright with ambition. Once they finally got home, she poured herself a stiff Jack Daniels and Coke while Gareth mixed his own martini. Another thing at which she was incompetent. He liked it dry, but not too dry. Who the hell knew what that meant?

After making his pronouncement on the foundation of their marriage, Gareth staggered off to bed, leaving Ellie to stare at the wall and contemplate the profundity of her errors in life.

Ellie shifted restlessly on the cot as rain rattled on the roof over her head. The problem was that he'd been such a handsome bastard. Clean-shaven, with a cleft chin and those damned dimples when he smiled. Slim, well groomed, and a smooth baritone voice that could charm a snake out of its basket. Or a woman out of her dress.

Unwillingly, Ellie remembered an evening when she'd

come home late after a long day running a crime scene as a newly minted detective sergeant in the Southern Georgian Bay detachment based in Midland.

This was Eleanor March at thirty-one years of age.

The commute between the detachment office and their apartment was an hour and forty-five minutes one way, but her gas and mileage were covered and she had decided against boarding in Midland, because she was determined not to be away from her girls, who were now six and two. Her job kept her away from home for long hours, however, which failed to please Gareth. Melanie and Megan were in the care of a housekeeper during the day and so were less and less affected by her absences, but a gap was growing between her and them that would eventually become irreparable.

On this particular night, she was exhausted. A gas bar and convenience store robbery that morning had gone terribly wrong. The store owner had tried to defend himself with a baseball bat against three young men with guns. There were more customers inside the store than the robbers realized, and seven people ended up dead, including the owner, three customers, two of the gunnies, and one cop. As it happened, a provincial constable had just pulled up to the pumps and was lifting the hose to fill his tank when he heard the shots inside. Drawing his sidearm, he burst inside and shot one of the hold-up men as he was gunning down two of the customers. The other man shot the constable, who returned fire and killed his assailant before succumbing to his wounds.

It was an awful mess.

Forensics spent hours determining how many shots had been fired, who exactly had shot whom, and where the rounds had all ended up. Surviving customers were in shock and had to be handled with care outside as Ident and the detectives worked inside with the coroner and EMS. Interviews stretched on into the afternoon, including the owner's wife, who lived in the apartment upstairs and had heard the whole thing.

As incident commander, Ellie had remained on the scene for the duration, keeping track of who came and went, assigning priorities to each step in the on-scene investigation, and making sure everyone stayed in the loop as far as what was being done and what was next.

When she finally made it back to the apartment, it was well after dark. The girls were in their bedroom, asleep, their door closed as usual, but Gareth was busy with a visitor in the living room.

Ellie had to pass through there in order to reach the bathroom. The visitor was a willowy blonde in a short black skirt and high heels. She and Gareth were bent over documents strewn across the coffee table, sorting through them, flank to flank.

"Eleanor," Gareth said, sparing a quick glance. "Didn't expect you home. This is Suzie. She's doing some clerical work for me."

"Hi," Suzie said tentatively.

Ellie continued on to the bathroom, where she closed the door, stripped, and took a long, hot shower. Fatigue and disappointment brought tears that were washed away by the sting of the water.

When she was done, she toweled herself off, put on a bathrobe hanging on the back of the door, and went into the bedroom.

Thankfully, the bed was still undisturbed.

She closed the door, turned off the light, slipped under the covers with her robe still on, and fell asleep.

On it went. She slept fitfully and awoke to a raging thirst. A bottle of water had been left beside the cot, and she drank it greedily.

Gareth. Damned Gareth. Now he was stuck in her head. Occasionally she dreamed about him, that they were still married and she was messing up something or other that pissed him off, but now it was like a wound she couldn't help rubbing.

Her head sank back on the pillow. She had to get out of here before Bruno decided she was too much trouble and killed her. She just couldn't summon the strength or the impetus to find a way out.

Gareth wanting out. Gareth walking out. His bag packed, a hotel room booked, he gave her a week to get her things together and leave. The apartment, a condominium actually, belonged to him and he wasn't going to give it up.

He declared that their settlement would be the model of simplicity. The girls would stay with him, of course, because she was unable to give them the care and attention they needed. He would keep the condo. He'd give her half their joint bank account, and he'd liquidate a third of his extensive stock portfolio and transfer the amount to her personal bank account.

She could take it or leave it. If she took it, then fine. They were done. If she left it, though, he'd fight her tooth and nail with the best attorney in the city. Her reputation as a failed mother would be dragged into the public, her record with the OPP would be gone over with a fine-tooth comb, et cetera, et cetera.

She took the deal.

Such a cold, cold man. She understood he'd never loved her. It was just difficult to accept that she'd read him so poorly at the beginning.

CHAPTER 45

Detective Inspector Kate Greene found her way to the second-floor meeting room of the Lanark County detachment office with the help of a secretary who babbled non-stop about the awful weather. Kate didn't reply, feeling that her appearance was answer enough.

They were sitting around the big table, waiting for her. She shook hands with Inspector Colleen Galvin, detachment commander; Staff Sergeant Gary Dunn, operations manager; Detective Sergeant Sonja Freeling, commander of the crime unit; and Detective Constables Walker, Woolfson, Hope, and Quinn.

"Wet weather we're having," Colleen remarked as she motioned to the vacant seat next to her.

She knew she looked a sight. Her coiled copper hair was plastered to her head like a mesh hair net. Her blue summer-weight jacket sagged and drooped, thoroughly soaked, and her shoes squished as she walked over and sat down. All of this had happened to her between the parking lot and the front entrance of the building. She felt like a drowned rat.

She set her briefcase down and opened it. Rivulets of water ran onto the table top. One of the detectives— Woolfson, it was—appeared at her elbow with a fistful of napkins and sopped it up for her.

"Sorry," she said, taking out her tablet and closing the lid. "It's just nuts out there."

Liam left the room and came back with a clean hand towel from his locker. Kate accepted it gratefully and used it to ruffle her hair.

"We're glad you're able to come down," Colleen said. "How was the drive?"

She pulled a strand of wet hair from the corner of her mouth. "Fine, until I got past Peterborough. But nothing like this, that's for sure. I take it you haven't heard anything from Ellie?"

Colleen looked at Sonja, who shook her head. "No, not a thing. Detective Constable Walker's taking the lead on this. Kevin, bring the inspector up to speed."

Kate looked at Quinn, realized her mistake, and shifted her attention to Kevin Walker. Although she was Ellie March's colleague as a detective inspector and major case manager, she normally worked Central Region and was not very familiar with personnel in Ellie's bailiwick. And since Ellie's disappearance was being treated as a kidnapping, and since kidnapping qualified as a major case in Ontario, she'd made the long drive down—four hours altogether in this weather—to meet these people and take up the reins of the investigation.

Kevin described the incident at the McDonald's as they understood it to have happened—the fender-bender; the assault on Ellie (she wouldn't have gone voluntarily); her motor pool vehicle left in the parking lot; CCTV showing the black Thunderbird leaving the scene; and the complete and total absence of communication from her since the incident.

Heather Hope then picked up the thread to explain the investigation into the rash of high-end auto thefts. Interviews with the victims had indicated a sophisticated and well-organized operation that used electronic devices on storage locks and keyless-entry car systems, along with very discreet scouting and execution.

They believed that the gang had a cooling spot somewhere in the area for temporary storage before the vehicles were containerized and shipped to the Port of Montreal for export overseas. This as-yet unknown location also likely doubled as a chop shop where less valuable vehicles were reduced to parts that would sell for more than the car or truck itself was worth.

It was the theft of the particular car mentioned by Kevin, a black 1964 Ford Thunderbird belonging to a local man named Alex Powell, that connected the auto theft ring to Ellie's disappearance.

"We believe she's being held at the cooling spot

location," Kevin said.

"And there's been no communication at all with these people?" Kate asked.

"None," Kevin said. "Complete silence."

"No demands for ransom, no threats to back off of them and their operation, nothing like that?"

"No. It's possible they don't know who she is. Her ID was in her bag in the Tahoe, and her firearm was stored in the centre console. The men who took her parked her vehicle in the McDonald's lot and left the keys in the ignition with the doors locked. If they'd tried the key to the centre console, they would have taken her gun and it wouldn't have been there for us to find."

"So she's just some random eyewitness to a car theft that they brought along to keep her quiet."

"She's probably invented some kind of cover story to avoid suspicion."

Kate smiled slightly, knowing Ellie well. "I imagine."

"But that's not necessarily a good thing, is it?" Liam asked. "If they knew she was a cop, they'd treat her differently than if she was just some housewife in the wrong place at the wrong time, wouldn't they?"

Kate's smile disappeared. "You may be right. Her life could be in grave danger."

"If they think she's disposable and not worth keeping around."

"Yes." She looked around the table. "Let's find that cooling spot forthwith, shall we?"

CHAPTER 46

Kevin emerged from the washroom and made his way down to his cubicle at the end of the corridor. When he'd first been assigned a workspace in the building, after coming into Lanark on loan from the Leeds County Crime Unit, they'd stuck him right across from the men's room, quite easily the worst spot in the building. After his transfer became permanent, however, Mr. McGregor, the office manager, had found him a better place. Thank goodness. McGregor had miraculously made it onto Kevin's Christmas list that holiday season.

Kevin was about to sit down when he heard a door slam somewhere nearby. *Really* slam. Someone was highly pissed. He waited a moment. Almost immediately, Sonja Freeling loomed in his doorway.

"You're driving."

"Okay."

Sonja turned around and put the heel of her boot

through the drywall. Twice.

Kevin hesitated, then put on his newsboy cap to protect his head from the rain. He led the way out into the parking lot.

Halfway to his car, Sonja stopped and let out a scream, followed by a somewhat unprofessional swear word Kevin had never heard her utter before.

"What's wrong, Sonja? Where are we going?"

"They stole it! The bastards!"

"Who? Stole what?"

"My Vette!" She screamed at him.

"From your place?"

"Right from my goddamned driveway! The bastards!"

"Get in. We're getting soaked."

Kevin did his best to calm her down on the half-hour drive from Perth to her home on the outskirts of Carleton Place. Heather and Liam were out tracking something down, and Farzan was on a conference call with his drug enforcement partners, so he was it.

He let her listen to the steady beat of the windshield wipers for several kilometers as she regained control of her breathing and reorganized her emotions. She was tough and experienced, and a very good sergeant, in Kevin's opinion. He knew the drive would buy her the time she needed to pull it together, so he kept his questions to himself and concentrated on the road in front of him, which was drenched with rainwater. Visibility was not very good, and he was aware that at any moment an unseen puddle could send him hydroplaning out of control. Which was the last thing Sonja needed as she wrestled with herself to lower her blood pressure and get her thoughts straightened out.

Tom Finnegan met them at the front door. He put his arm around Sonja and moved her into the foyer, nodding at Kevin over her shoulder. In the living room, a uniformed patrol officer waited for them, notebook out. According to the metal bar pinned to his shirt, his name was Pond. Since he worked out of the Carleton Place detachment office, he was unfamiliar to Kevin.

"We received the call from Mr. Finnegan at 14:56 hours," he said, "and I arrived here at 15:13. I took a verbal statement, which I guess you'll want him to go over again for you."

"What was your twenty when you got the call out?"

"Just outside Appleton."

"Figures," Sonja muttered.

"Please dear," Finnegan said, "sit down and let Kevin handle it."

"I *am* letting him handle it," she grumbled, dropping into an armchair and folding her arms.

"Thanks," Kevin said. Appleton was a few kilometers northeast of town, and the thieves would have driven her car in the opposite direction to take it to their cooling spot in Perth. Wherever it was. And assuming this was the same crew they were already chasing. Hence Sonja's disappointment that the patrol officer wouldn't have caught a glimpse of the vehicle while en route to her home.

As distant a chance as that might have been, anyway.

"Do you have any more questions, Constable Pond?"

Kevin asked.

"Not at the moment."

"You don't need to hang around. Don't forget to forward me a copy of your report."

When Pond was gone, Sonja stood up and began to pace. "Run me through it," she told her husband.

"Sonja," Kevin said. "My room. My interview."

She stared at him for a moment before nodding. "I'll be in the kitchen. I'll make some coffee. Want some?"

"Sure." Kevin sat down across from Finnegan. "All right, Tom. Run me through it." He and Finnegan were well acquainted, having met through Sonja when she took command of the crime unit several years ago.

Finnegan glanced over his shoulder in the direction of the kitchen before responding. "Don't hold it against her. That damned car's been her special project for the last two years. She rebuilt it from the ground up."

"I won't. Tell me what you can about the theft."

"I've been working at home this week. We're producing a new critical minerals strategy as a horizontal initiative with Industry, and I wanted some peace and quiet to focus on our senior analysts' work."

Kevin knew a little about the situation regarding critical minerals in Canada, having followed recent news on the subject. The movement toward clean energy technologies, for example, would require dependable supplies of lithium, nickel, and copper, among other minerals, and the federal government wanted to ensure that Canada had a strong strategy focusing on mining, manufacturing, and efficient supply chains. It would seem that Sonja's husband was at the forefront of all this government work.

"That's right," Kevin said. "You were promoted last fall, weren't you?"

"Yeah, God help me. Senior director of Strategic and Horizontal Policy."

"But still in Natural Resources Canada, right?"

Finnegan nodded. "Which explains why I'm here instead of at my office. I ran out of milk for my tea, so I drove down to the convenience store to pick some up. I was gone fifteen minutes, tops. Which explains why I *wasn't* here when the car was taken."

"Which explains why *your* car's in the driveway instead of the Corvette," Sonja said, returning from the kitchen with a tray.

"I'm so very sorry, love," he said, accepting a cup and saucer.

"Don't be silly." She let Kevin take his coffee and said, "How's that for great timing? Gone in sixty seconds, eh?"

Kevin nodded, getting her point. The crew must have had the Corvette under active surveillance just as Finnegan left, giving them a wide-open opportunity to boost it. He hated to ask the question, but he did.

"Was it locked, Sonja?"

"Yes, Kevin."

"What year is it?"

"It's a 1963. One of the most desirable Vettes out there. It was a piece of junk when I bought it. Only the paint job was still good. The engine was totally blown."

"What's it worth?"

"I'd say about a hundred and ten."

"Thousand?"

She nodded. "It's got the split rear window, which is relatively hard to find these days. I paid fifty for it and put another thirty into it."

"Thousand."

"Yes, Kevin. Thousand."

Holy crap. Kevin digested this bit of news for a moment. "Tom, have you noticed any unusual activity on the street over the last week or so?"

He thought for a moment. "Not unusual, no. A bit more traffic than we ordinarily get, I thought, but then again it's been a while since I've been here during the day."

The Finnegan-Freeling home was located on Lake Park Road at the intersection of a quiet side road, south of the town limits of Carleton Place and within easy reach of Highway 7. It was a beautiful property, featuring four bedrooms, three bathrooms, a walk-out basement, a fire pit, and a large deck off the living room. A tall privacy fence enclosed the back yard, but the front driveway was fully visible, due in large part to the fact it was a corner lot. Kevin had already noticed several vantage points from which the thieves could have kept an eye on their candy apple prize.

"I'm surprised," Finnegan said, "that they'd take a car during a storm like this. Wouldn't that be more risky?"

"It probably provided them better cover," Kevin said. "Fewer people outdoors; fewer potential eyewitnesses."

Sonja made a fist. "Find my damned car, Kevin."

"Let's find that cooling spot," he replied. "Chances are, it'll be there."

CHAPTER 47

Ellie had no idea what time it was when the door opened and Squid walked in, pistol in hand, venom in his eyes.

She sat up. "So this is it?"

His lip curled. "Where do you want it, bitch? Head or heart?"

"Now there's a choice."

Squid racked a round into the chamber.

It was a Walther PDP, Ellie saw. "Nine or forty?"

"What the hell do you care?"

He slowly levelled the gun at her, sideways, the way a gang punk would hold it.

"Squid. Wait."

It was Junior. He stepped aside in the doorway. Bruno rolled past him.

"Put that away," he hissed, wheeling up to Ellie's cot.

Another form filled the doorway. A tall man, his London Fog trench coat dark with rain, his black fedora dripping. "Bruno, move out of the way."

As the wheelchair rolled aside, Ellie watched the man remove his hat and shake the water from it.

It was Leonardo Arcuri.

"You," she said.

Leonardo closed his eyes. He rubbed his forehead, sighed deeply, and cleared his throat. His next words were to Bruno: "What in the name of God were you thinking?"

"She got tangled up with the goofballs, like I said on the phone. They brought her here until we figured out what to do with her."

"And you have no idea who this is?"

"She said her name was Eleanor something."

"March," Junior supplied. "A housecleaner."

Leonardo glared at him. "Silence. Do not speak again."

"I don't understand the problem, sir," Bruno murmured.

"*Per amore di Gesù*, she's *polizia*. An inspector. Very important."

Ellie saw the shock in Bruno's eyes as Leonardo's words registered. "Oh my God, we didn't know. She said—"

"Silence. Leave us alone."

The room quickly emptied. Junior closed the door gently behind him, as though afraid of even the slightest sound.

"Ellie, Ellie, Ellie. I'm so sorry. What have they done?"

He stripped off his trench coat and draped it over the desk chair with his hat. He dragged over the stool and sat down.

"You came just in time. I was about to be disappeared."

"Idiots. Fools. I'll have their balls on a dinner plate for my dogs to eat."

"You're the last person I expected to see here, Leonardo."

"I was returning to Vaughan from a meeting in Ottawa. The weather is so horrible, I told the driver to stop here. Anyway, I wanted to check on this hostage the morons were holding." He studied her face. "They've beaten you."

"A misunderstanding."

"You tried to escape?"

"Yeah. Bad idea."

"Drugs?"

"Some kind of sedative."

"I can see it in your eyes." He leaned forward, resting his forearms on his thighs. "Tell me something, Ellie. Were you targeting us?"

She made a rude noise. "I was going home. Just bought supper for my dog and me when your boys crossed a lane and hit me."

"*Christo.*" He lowered his head. "I'm trying to think of a way out of this."

"How about I arrest the whole damn lot of you and get my phone returned to me so I can call for backup?"

"I'd prefer something less disastrous for myself,

personally."

"Not sure I can help you with that." Ellie swung around and lay down, resting her head on the pillow. "I thought you . . . said you didn't have any business in this area."

"That was in reference to human trafficking, Ellie. I spoke the truth. We don't get involved with that whatsoever. Other families do, maybe, but not this one. It's dehumanizing and repulsive to me. Human beings are not cattle. When Peter Humbert met his unfortunate end, it wasn't because someone thought he was encroaching on our business. It's because they hated what he was doing and what he stood for."

The owner of a chain of pizzerias and laundromats between Kingston and Port Hope along the Saint Lawrence Seaway, Humbert had led an alt-right organization known as the Freedom Defenders, an anti-vaccination, anti-government, white supremacist group trying to involve themselves in a range of criminal activities to feed their bank accounts. When an OPP provincial constable was murdered by one of Humbert's associates, the resultant investigation rolled up a local family tied to the Freedom Defenders. News came later that Humbert had been gunned down in a parking lot in Cobourg. Leonardo's 'Ndrangheta organization had been suspected of carrying out the hit, but nothing was ever proven.

And now?

"They wouldn't . . . let me see anything, but it's obviously a stolen car ring. You're running it, I suppose."

He shook his head. "More like a franchise. They pay

a fee and get to work a territory that runs from Ottawa to Kingston. I shouldn't be telling you this."

"Yes, you should."

"It's your irresistible charm, Ellie. I'm very fond of you, you know."

"Don't start."

"The sedative is taking effect."

"Yeah."

He stood up suddenly, retrieving his coat and hat. "I have to get out of here before the weather gets even worse. I'm closing this place down. It may take a day or two. Then they'll release you and vanish. It's the best I can offer."

Ellie said nothing, her eyes closed.

"You'll do what you have to do," Leonardo said, moving to the door, "but always remember this. I owe you a debt for what has happened here. No matter the outcome. It's an obligation, a point of honour. Arcuri owes you compensation."

Ellie heard him close the door behind him, and then she was alone.

CHAPTER 48

Heather wanted to do a drive-by of a place out on Scotch Line Road, a couple of kilometers southwest of the town limits. It showed up on Google Maps as a roadside gas bar with a large warehouse-sized building behind it, but further research revealed that the gas bar had been closed for several years and the property was vacant and unused. It could be a good front for their cooling spot, she believed.

Liam offered to drive, but Heather waved him off. Although the rain was coming down in sheets, she was focused on the possibility she'd found the place they were looking for. She wanted to be the one in control of the discovery.

She had changed into a fresh T-shirt that he had noticed under her lightweight OPP rain jacket. It featured large and colourful rectangles with "Pow!" "Bam!" and

"Kapow!" Bat-fight words reminiscent of the old *Batman* television show.

"Nice tee," he said.

"Mmm." She leaned forward, peering through the windshield at the street that showed up intermittently in front of them between the beating of the wipers.

"How come you don't like my jokes?"

"Hmmm? They're corny."

"I was under the impression you liked corny stuff. Offbeat stuff."

She said nothing, maneuvering carefully around a corner.

"I must have been wrong."

Heather turned the wipers up to their highest speed. "You weren't wrong."

"When I was in high school, a teacher asked me a question and I answered with a joke. He knew my reputation as a class clown, but it rubbed him the wrong way, so he hauled me up in front of the class and ordered me to do a one-liner routine and not to stop until he said so.

"Great, I thought, and off I went. At first the class went nuts, because some of my gags were pretty good, but it went on for a long time and eventually I started getting tired and the jokes got lamer. My legs started to shake from standing for so long. It was really long. Finally, one of the kids said, 'Don't you think it's enough? You should let him sit down now.'

"The teacher looked at me and said, 'What do you think, Liam. Had enough?' I looked right back at him and said, 'I've had enough of this shampoo. I want real poo.'"

Heather barked a short laugh.

"See? I'm just a funny guy."

"Did he let you sit down?"

"He was too busy looking at the blackboard and choking on a grin. I just went back to my seat, thinking, 'To hell with you, pal.' It's like most other things in life, Heather. I can take whatever they dish out."

Heather drove past the place she was looking for and had to turn around and come back. The gas bar was as advertised, a derelict shack needing to be torn down. The shingles on the roof were flapping in the wind like birds trying to shake their tethers. She drove around to the back and eased up in front of the warehouse.

It was fairly large, a single-storey building with three bay doors in front. There was no signage to indicate who owned it or what it might have been used for. It looked as abandoned as the gas bar. Trees on either side waved in the gale-force wind, their branches bobbing up and down.

The rain had eliminated any possibility of seeing tire tracks leading in and out of the big doors. Heather's hopes dimmed, but she shoved the gearshift into park and unbuckled her seat belt.

"I want to take a look inside."

"I'll come with you," Liam said, removing his own belt.

"Wait here. No sense two of us getting soaked."

She opened her door and stepped out. Before her body was clear, a violent gust slammed the door back against her. She gasped and swore, pushing against it to free herself. As soon as she was out, the wind slammed it shut. She dropped to one knee, pain searing her hip and leg.

Liam was suddenly there, kneeling beside her, an arm around her shoulder. "Are you all right? Let me help you up."

She shrugged him off and hobbled to the closest bay door. Cupping her hands to her temples, she peered inside.

There was jack squat to see. A couple of hoists, one halfway elevated; dirt and debris everywhere; a few tables along the wall littered with parts, empty cartons, and garbage; a bird, likely a starling, flying back and forth.

"Shit," she yelled against the howling of the wind.

Liam grabbed her by the shoulders. "Back to the car!"

They started forward, but gusts of wind threatened to take them off their feet. A branch broke off one of the trees and came right at them.

He shoved her forward as it landed on him, knocking him down and covering him.

"Liam!" Heather screamed.

He pushed the branch aside. "I'm okay!" he shouted. "Missed me by that much!"

Back in the car, Heather leaned over the steering wheel and sobbed for a brief moment.

Liam finger-combed his dripping hair away from his face. "Are you okay?"

"Me? Am I okay? You're the one who nearly got brained by Mother Nature!"

"I'm okay. In fact, I feel *tree*-mendous! Know what I should have said to that branch back there? Leaf me alone! What kind of tree grows on your hand? A palm tree!"

She laughed and cried at the same time, rain dripping from her chin, as she reached out and gripped his arm. "You dear, sweet bonehead. You can crack your corny jokes whenever the hell you want!"

She leaned over and kissed him, hard.

CHAPTER 49

As soon as Leonardo was gone, the woman came in and forced Ellie to drink a cup of cold coffee with a bitter aftertaste. Why would they continue to drug her? Hadn't Leonardo said she would be released soon?

She lay there listening to the clamour and chaos in the rest of the building, audible over the howling of the wind and the rattling of sheet metal trying to tear itself off the roof. The work to obey Leonardo's orders to break down the operation and make it disappear was apparently well underway.

Bangs and crashes; engines being started and revved; bay doors clattering open long enough to allow trucks to enter with containers for the vehicles. She pictured it all, her eyes closed, her mind beginning to swirl as the sedative took effect once more.

For some reason, she thought of her girls, Melanie and Megan. She thought of birthday gifts she'd bought for them that they'd thrown in the garbage. Mean things they'd said to her. Their naked hatred of her. Her suspicion that it was all stoked by Gareth to draw them closer to him and to Suzie, the new love-object in his life.

She'd long since put the emotions behind her. She'd accepted the fact that her family had moved on without her. It didn't control her life. It didn't even affect her all that much, not after this long. The guilt was residual, like coffee grounds at the bottom of the cup.

She thought of Justin Paige, who'd lost his daughter in a very different way. Not through alienation and estrangement, but through murder. He'd taken it very hard. So hard, in fact, that he'd tried to kill himself by jumping off the same cliff that had taken his daughter's life.

At the hospital, Ellie had stood by his bedside, putting her emotions away and regarding him with the objectivity of a law enforcement officer. She was mildly surprised at how easily she was able to do it. She felt empathy for the man, and sadness, but didn't allow the feelings to remain in the forefront of her thinking as she catalogued his injuries.

Fractured skull; broken pelvis; broken arms; and a broken leg. Lacerations and contusions. Internal injuries that were not judged to be life-threatening. He was in traction, and it would take a long time for the injuries to heal. After that would be a long course of physiotherapy. All of it dependent, of course, on whether or not there was brain damage. He was unconscious, but scans were negative. They wouldn't know for sure, though, until he woke up.

She'd been dozing. She woke up and shivered. So cold. The temperature had taken such an incredible nosedive.

Paige hadn't lived to see her break the case. His heart had stopped only seven hours after she and Brand had been at the hospital to check on him. He died not knowing what had happened to Cindy, and who was responsible.

Father and daughter were buried side by side in the United Church cemetery in Fergus.

SEPTEMBER 2002

CHAPTER 50

Ellie was returning from a washroom break when her desk phone rang.

"Eleanor March."

"Eleanor, this is Jeremiah in Ident."

"Oh, hi, Dan. How are you doing?"

"Not bad. Your print checks came back. on William Orton and Dawn Paige."

"Oh, great. Could you fax them over?"

"Already running through the machine. Just wanted to give you a heads up. And to let you know you just rang the bell."

"Really?"

"Lunch is on you, my dear."

She hung up and walked around to the fax machine, which was located in a cubicle next to Sergeant Morrow's office. It was still whirring as another page of flimsy paper worked its way through its guts.

There were four sheets in the hopper so far. She picked them up. The top one was a cover memo for the search conducted on prints collected from William Steven Orton, and the next two were the basic form that had been created from lifts of Orton's fingerprints. The memo stated that his identity was confirmed, and a criminal record check came back negative. Orton was clean, as far as his past was concerned.

Ellie flicked to the fourth sheet, which was the covering memo on Dawn Paige's handprint. Her eyes moved to the second paragraph, where the results were summarized for easy reference.

Her heart nearly stopped.

The fingerprints belonged to Anna Leigh Dombrowski, DOB 1966/4/21, place of birth Winnipeg, MB.

What the hell?

She waited impatiently as the rest of the fax squeezed out into the hopper. When she had the complete document, she found the statement relating to chain of custody. There was no doubt about it. The scenes-of-crime officer and the forensic technician, Identification Constable Dan Jeremiah, had signed off on the description of how the handprints had been lifted from the table in the interview room immediately after the departure of Dawn Paige, that the latents had been transferred to the lab while following all approved protocols, et cetera, et cetera.

These were Dawn Paige's prints.

Dawn Paige was Anna Leigh Dombrowski.

Ellie sat down in a nearby chair.

Anna Leigh Dombrowski was one of Canada's most notorious female serial killers. Working with her partner, the man she'd referred to in her interview with Ellie as Terry Aldress—whose real name was Gerald Roger Alcorn—she had participated in a series of sexual homicides between 1985 and 1989.

The six victims were all nurses at Brandon General Hospital, Ellie recalled, where Anna Leigh had taken a job as part of the janitorial staff. Four were RNs and two were student nurses she befriended. After winning their trust, she convinced them to come home with her to meet her boyfriend, who worked in television.

The details of the case had played out across the media for most of that year. Alcorn in fact did work in television. He was a studio cameraman with Channel 5 in Brandon, a CBC affiliate. He'd brought equipment home from work and set it up in their spare bedroom, which they used as a "play room," as he called it during interrogation. They took turns watching through the camera while the other performed, the whole vile thing being recorded for their later titillation.

As it turned out, when they finished with their victims Alcorn strangled them. Bundling them up in bedding, they loaded them into his van and drove them to an isolated spot on the Assiniboine River west of the city, where Alcorn cut off their hands and decapitated them. The body went into the river, and the parts were buried in burlap sacks nearby.

They were caught in June 1989 when one of the nurses revived while being put into the van. She escaped and was able to contact police. Anna Leigh negotiated a plea deal, convincing authorities she was coerced by Alcorn into cooperating with him and providing testimony to convict him. She received an eight-year sentence and was released in January 1998. She immediately disappeared.

Changing her name to Dawn Smith—as Ellie figured out later, putting the pieces together—she hitched a ride to Ontario and met Justin Paige more or less as she'd described. She started a new life, hiding out as a simple housewife and janitor in another province under two other names—Smith and Paige—but apparently she hadn't left her violent behaviour behind. Although Cindy's autopsy had managed to rule out any form of sexual assault, Anna Leigh had clearly added another notch to her belt, as far as Ellie was concerned.

She ran to Brand's cubicle and told him the news.

"Get us a warrant," she said. "I'm going to break her. She killed Cindy."

"Eleanor—"

"She's mine, Leif. She's all mine."

CHAPTER 51

They showed up at Orton's two-bedroom home shortly after 11:00 PM, the warrants finally having arrived to arrest Dawn Paige/Anna Leigh Dombrowski and William Steven Orton. They also had warrants to search the house, to search both vehicles and take tire tread impressions to match those collected at the Paige home and the trail parking area, and to seize all their footwear for comparison to prints they'd gathered.

Ellie's heart was pounding like a Porsche flat-six engine at high rev, but her face was impassive as Orton opened the door in his pajamas and stepped back, shocked. In a matter of moments the little house was filled with law enforcement, as uniformed constables, SOCOs, identification constables, and Brand fanned out into the rooms and began to work.

Orton was hustled into the bathroom with his clothes in his arms and ordered to dress under the watchful eye of an officer, after having received notification of his arrest on suspicion of having conspired to murder Cindy Paige. He sputtered and swore, demanding a lawyer, until Brand stepped in to describe what happened to men in prison who killed teenaged girls. It was pure fiction, but it did the trick, turning Orton's aggression into a weeping declaration that he had no idea what Dawn had done to her ex-step-daughter. As he tugged at his zipper, the constable took him by the arm and hustled him outside, still barefoot, and put him into the back of a cruiser.

Dawn was still in bed when Ellie went into the bedroom. She was sitting up, propped up against her pillows, a sheet only half-covering her nakedness. A female constable moved Ellie aside and went to the closet, pulling a T-shirt and jeans from hangers and tossing them onto the bed. Dawn had already been informed, like her boyfriend, of the reasons for her arrest. She was just grandstanding now, as far as Ellie was concerned.

"Don't make me dress you myself," the constable growled, reminding Ellie of herself at that stage of her career.

Dawn slowly rose from the bed and retrieved a pair of panties from a dresser drawer, flaunting the body that had made her a subject of such interest with so many men. Ellie rolled her eyes and looked over her shoulder at a SOCO standing in the doorway.

"Five minutes," she snapped at him. "Get lost."

When Dawn was dressed, Ellie cuffed her hands behind her back and led her out of the bedroom. The SOCO brushed past them without a glance. A constable met her in the hallway and took charge of the prisoner.

Dawn stopped in the doorway. "This is a complete waste of time," she said to Ellie. "You can't prove a thing."

"You'll find out what we can prove. Move it."

"It's too bad, sister. You're a hard worker and you mean well, but I've seen it all before. You won't put me away."

The look in her cold dead eyes would stay with Ellie for the rest of her life.

CHAPTER 52

To Ellie's disappointment, Dawn Paige/Anna Leigh Dombrowski would not be hers after all. The interrogation wouldn't be conducted by Leif Brand, either. Or Detective Inspector Carol Duncan, for that matter.

The Criminal Investigation Branch decided instead to send down their best interrogator, Detective Sergeant Jim Waterfield. He had a long list of successful cases to his credit, including a missing girl murdered by her mother and buried in the woods; a commissioned officer in the Canadian Armed Forces who preyed on women living near the base where he was stationed; and a serial killer who hitch-hiked from town to town in the northern part of the province.

While Anna Leigh was made comfortable in the interview room, Duncan and Waterfield conferred in the hallway. Once their watches were synchronized, as it were, Waterfield took his place across the table from their suspect, and Duncan came into the video room to observe.

The chair she settled into, directly in front of the monitor, was next to the one occupied by Ellie. Duncan had insisted she be included, recognizing the lengths to which Ellie had gone to bring the case this far. She also wanted an opportunity to get a sense of who Ellie was as a professional and to offer a bit of coaching if she thought Ellie would be receptive.

Ellie was definitely receptive.

She watched Waterfield begin slowly, establishing up front that Dawn Paige was willing to acknowledge her true identity as Anna Leigh Dombrowski. It was an important first hurdle for a couple of reasons. First, it helped establish a baseline of truthfulness. Second, it obviated the necessity of beating around the bush with fingerprints, chain of custody, lab reliability, and all the other pitfalls that could delay or derail the case. Anna Leigh confidently admitted that she was the notorious Brandon serial killer's reluctant accomplice.

With that out of the way, Waterfield wanted to move things on to Cindy Paige, but Anna Leigh wasn't done talking about her past. She pointed out that she'd done her time, that she'd served her debt to society, and that she now deserved to be left alone to live the rest of her life in peace and quiet.

"Jim's patient," Duncan said to Ellie. "He's trying to get a sense of whether or not she's carrying a burden of guilt over what happened to Cindy. He'll lay the groundwork by making her feel that she has a choice. She can talk to him if she wants to, get it off her chest. It'll take him a while to get to that point."

"She's tough," Ellie said. "Hard-headed."

"I can see that."

Waterfield spent almost an hour satisfying Anna Leigh's desire to talk about her Manitoba past. Initially, she floated the image of a young woman taken advantage of by older, more cynical men with only one thing on their mind, but Waterfield firmly let her know that he wasn't buying it. Eventually, she dropped that pose and went back to her earlier refrain that she'd paid her debt and had a right to privacy that was being denied by all this harassment over the death of her ex-husband's little bitch daughter.

Now that she'd finally moved to the present case, Waterfield shifted gears and went after her with a long, unrelenting pressure to tell the truth about what had happened. He talked about her car's tire tread marks having been found in the Paige driveway. A well-known antipathy between her and the girl. Her inability to account for her whereabouts that day.

Anna Leigh fended off the high-pressure tactics as though waving at an annoying fly buzzing around her face. She asked Waterfield if they'd found her tire tracks at the hiking trail parking area. The detective deflected the question, knowing that Constable Dearborn had failed to extract a positive match from fragments collected at the crime scene. She asked if he had any eyewitnesses who could place her there at the time of Cindy's death. Again, she seemed to be able to sense instinctively another hole in their case.

Duncan leaned over. "He's studying her emotional profile. He's listening to her tone of voice and her volume, the pacing of her speech, her diction—word choice—and also non-verbals like eye contact, what she's doing with her hands, her posture. So many indicators to keep track of. Jim's the best, but I'm wondering if he may have met his match this time."

"She's not giving him anything to work with," Ellie said.

"No, she's not. I don't think I've ever seen a suspect exercise as much self-control as this woman is right now. She's as solid as a rock. He won't get a confession. He just won't."

"Damn," Ellie whispered.

"We'll just have to get out there and work the physical evidence all over again," Duncan said. "There's no time for anger and frustration." She held up a finger. "Focus. Like a laser beam. We need to match her intensity, her focus, her complete mastery of her emotions."

"Yes, ma'am."

"Don't call me that. Call me Carol."

"Yes, ma'am. Carol."

PRESENT DAY

Kate Greene's composure restored and her clothing and hair now merely damp and uncomfortable, she felt ready to sit in on the video conference call to which she'd been summoned. It was a command performance—also on the line with her were her boss, Gavin Elliott; Chief Superintendent Jordan Malcolmsen, commander of the East Region; and the Supreme Leader, Commissioner Cecil Dart.

Dart was an imposing figure. His white hair was a closely trimmed cap around a receding hairline, and his face had the weathered look of an old catcher's mitt that had been left outside all winter. His eyes were dark and brooding. His mouth was a tight, lipless line.

"Kate," he said, his voice sounding like tires on a gravel driveway, "take me through an honest assessment of her situation. Is it your sense that Ellie would have done everything she could to hide her identity from these people?"

"Yes, sir. It's a scenario where she was an inadvertent witness to a high-end auto theft, and the suspects would have taken her with them thinking it would prevent her from identifying them to the police."

"And you haven't heard a word from them. No calls with ransom demands or threats, nothing like that."

"Correct, sir."

"You say you believe she's being held in a warehouse in the area that's part of their operation."

"Yes, sir."

"Jordan, you need to flood the area with resources and find this place, ASAP."

Malcolmsen cleared his throat. "We're doing what we can, but it's pure chaos down here. Right now the province has declared it a Major Event, but we'll have to see if it's upgraded from there."

Dart winced. "Yeah. Okay. I understand. But just the same, nothing must happen to Ellie. They may decide she's disposable and . . ."

"We're doing everything we can, sir," Kate said.

"I'm sure you are. Keep me informed." His conference call window flipped to black.

Gavin Elliott rubbed his mouth. "Kate, I promise I'll contribute to your Go Fund Me campaign while you're looking for a new job."

"Thanks, Gav."

"There are just no other resources to be had right now," Malcolmsen said. "I hate to say it, but that's the reality we have to face."

"We understand, Jordan."

"If there's nothing else, sirs," Kate said, "I'll get back to work."

"Best of luck," Gavin said.

She signed off and decided to go downstairs to see what the crime unit team had come up with. *Do you believe in miracles?*

No, she thought. *But this time I might make an exception.*

CHAPTER 54

Alaric Quinn removed his glasses and began to polish them. "Heather called in to say that their location is a bust. They've gone to ground until the weather lets up a bit."

"That's another one off the list," Kate Greene said. "What's next?"

"I'm open to suggestions," Kevin said, staring at the map on the big screen.

Aydin Farzan stood in the doorway, arms folded. "I'm not sure if this means anything."

Sonja Freeling—who'd recovered sufficiently from having almost swallowed her tongue over the theft of her beloved Corvette to be able to get back to work—gestured him in. "What is it, Aydin?"

Farzan walked up to the screen. "I'm renting a house on South Street, right across from the fire department. Here." He pointed. "I've been there, what, a month and a half so far? Anyway, one of the things I've noticed about Perth is that there are a lot of really nice cars in town. I'm not sure where people get the money to afford them sometimes. The other day I saw a Lamborghini, which surprised me."

Kate Greene frowned. "Really?"

"Yeah. Beautiful car. Then the day after that I saw an orange Porsche, a vintage Targa. I thought there must be some kind of auto club in the area. Rich guys showing off their rides to each other. Now I'm wondering if it's connected to your investigation."

Kevin joined him at the screen. "Show me where you saw them."

Farzan moved his finger. "This is South Street." He tapped. "This is my house. And right here," he pointed, "is the intersection at Rogers Road. Just a couple doors up from me. This is where I saw them."

"Which way were they going?"

"The Porsche was travelling east past my house. I watched it turn right onto Rogers. It went down here." He moved his finger in a southerly direction. "The Lambo was on Rogers, and went straight through the intersection. South."

"What's down there, Alaric?" asked Kevin.

"It's an industrial area right at the far end of town. There's a car wash; uh, a glass business, windows and that kind of stuff; the distillery where Jane Ledbetter's BMW was stolen—Heather and Liam talked to her—and a few warehouses—"

The power went off.

Heather's laptop beeped and died.

"Damn," Alaric said, "we need a battery backup in this room."

Staff Sergeant Dunn stuck his head in. "Everyone all right in here?"

"We're fine," Kate said.

"Emergency power should kick in pretty soon."

Kevin stood up. "Staff, can you get me a backup team in the next twenty minutes or so?"

"Everybody's already out, Kevin, because of the storm. Cars in the ditch, trees coming down, blocking streets. It's wild out there."

The emergency power system kicked in, and Alaric brought Heather's laptop back to life.

"We've got a tentative location on Ellie," Kevin said.

"I'll free someone up for you. Where?"

"Here." Kevin showed him on the screen, which displayed their map once again. "This industrial park at the foot of Rogers."

"As soon as you know for sure, call me. I'll get someone to you."

Kevin looked at Sonja.

"Go," she said.

CHAPTER 55

After grabbing his rain jacket and hat from his cubicle, Kevin hurried out the rear exit into the parking lot. The wind hit him like a sheet of plywood torn from a wall. He staggered off balance. His hat went flying across the parking lot.

He groaned. Janie would be upset if he lost it. The urgency of the situation forced him to step toward his car. He *had* to get down to Rogers Road soonest! The hat fetched up against the wheel of a car. Clenching his teeth, he changed direction and hurried after it.

Tossing it into the back seat of his car, he threw an emergency flashing red light onto the dashboard and peeled out of the parking lot. Normally it would only take about ten minutes or so to drive from the north end of town to the south end, depending on the time of day and the traffic, but Kevin was forced to slow down, as the buffeting crosswinds threatened to roll his car at each intersection.

He saw a downed hydro pole on a cross-street, sparks flashing, and an OPP cruiser blocking the way while a hydro crew assessed the damage, their bright yellow-and-silver rain gear shimmering as water streaked across his passenger window.

Two blocks later, a tree had split in half and was obstructing traffic. No crew had arrived yet to work on clearing it; presumably everyone was currently busy elsewhere. A car had stopped in front of it, but the people inside were wisely staying where they were instead of getting out to gawk.

Kevin took an immediate right and found himself at Rogers Road. He turned left and gunned it, swerving around cars pulled over to the curb trying to outwait the storm. He reached South Street, paused, and raced through.

Where was she? Where? Where?

Look for a chop shop, he told himself. Shipping containers outside; maybe cars in the lot; maybe heavy equipment for moving the containers from a truck onto the ground and vice versa. A discreet but busy enterprise. A place employing a crew of mechanics, forklift operators, logistics specialists, and thieves with dangerous temperaments.

He crept past the glass business, wipers on high, fan blasting air up onto the windshield, which insisted on fogging up because of the humidity.

Christ! He ducked instinctively as a tree branch struck the hood of his car and bounced away. His heart pounded as he swallowed the adrenaline and pressed onward.

He passed the car wash, which was closed down and deserted.

He reached the driveway of a smallish warehouse. The sign out front identified it as belonging to J.T. Logistics. He pulled in and began to circle the building.

At the rear was a single bay door and a staircase leading up to a steel man door with a small window in it. As he slowed for a look, the steel door opened and a woman waved out at him, likely drawn out by the flashing light on his dash. It wasn't Ellie. She yelled something. He held his hand to his ear, little finger and thumb extended in the familiar "call me" gesture. *Call 911*, he mouthed.

The wind shoved her back inside, and the door abruptly slammed.

He left this warehouse behind and rolled on toward the next.

Down at the end of the street, a vehicle emerged from another lot and turned toward him. In front of the building it had just left, it stopped abruptly as a sheet of metal roofing flew out of nowhere, slicing through the driver's window and lodging in the windshield from the inside. The vehicle veered crazily and smashed into a utility pole.

Kevin hurried down and got out, staggering against the wind. He started for the driver's side door but the steel sheet was blocking access, so he circled the vehicle, which was a newish black Range Rover, and tried the passenger side.

The door opened. Kevin looked in at a head sitting on the passenger seat in a pool of blood. Moments ago it had belonged to a mixed-race male who wore his hair in long, dark dreadlocks. His open eyes were brown, and at the last instant of life they had registered extreme surprise. His goatee was soaked with blood.

Kevin slammed the door and lurched back to his car. He hurried down to the warehouse from which the Range Rover had driven out. As he turned in the driveway, an enormously violent gust tore a portion of the roof off and flung it away, taking part of the wall and an emergency exit door with it.

A figure staggered out, was caught by the wind, and tumbled across the lot.

Kevin jumped out of the car and ran forward.

CHAPTER 56

Breakfast had been late. When Junior finally arrived, he handed her an apple and said that much of the building had already been cleared out, the people scattered and gone. He didn't say where. He told her that a bit later, he would take her out somewhere not far from town and drop her off with her cellphone. That was the plan, anyway. And they'd never see each other again.

"That's what you think," Ellie said.

He left without reacting, too stressed to catch her meaning. That she'd see him again at his trial. The door slammed shut.

Ellie didn't hear the key in the lock.

Her head had cleared a bit without the morning dose of drugs. She could almost think straight again. Almost.

The room was cold, and she was shivering. She took a bite of the apple and tossed it aside. The walls began to shake as the wind howled. She heard someone shouting above the racket.

All of a sudden a corner of the ceiling peeled back with a groan. She could see daylight. Debris and rain poured through the opening, rattling and banging around the room. Something struck her head and something else smashed against her leg.

She had to get the hell out of there.

She ran to the door and tried it. It opened! She'd been right; Junior hadn't locked it behind him when he left. Probably so that she might have a chance to escape and save her own life, if the disintegrating building didn't kill her first.

She stumbled into the corridor and tripped over junk, splintered pieces of wood, chunks of drywall, sodden masses of pink insulation, doors ripped from their hinges. Her ears buzzed from the air pressure and the incredible roaring of the wind. Her head spun as she half-ran and half-staggered, still shaking off the light-headedness that lingered from the sedatives.

She made it into the main garage area, but all three bay doors were damaged beyond use. Cars were tumbled everywhere. Wildly, she looked around for a possible way out. Where the hell could she go?

Unbelievably, as though the universe wished to test her beyond normal human endurance, Squid appeared in front of her. Blood flowed from a laceration on his scalp and another on his right cheek. His bristly hair was soaked, as were his clothes.

He saw her and drew his gun. It was the same Walther

he'd been about to kill her with before Leonardo had thankfully intervened. He leered, shook blood from his eyes, and raised his weapon, determined not to be denied this time around.

His arm trembled, and Ellie noticed that his shirtsleeve was red just under the shoulder around a jagged tear. Rivulets of blood coursed out from under the cuff of his sleeve and dripped off the edge of his hand. Snarling, he gripped his wrist with his free hand to steady his aim.

Ellie stooped quickly, grabbed a piece of two-by-four, and swung with all her might, striking his hands. The gun flew away, disappearing into the deluge.

Squid shrieked, bending over to cradle what must have been a broken wrist or two. He looked up at her.

Her lip curling in a snarl, she swung again from the heels and struck him squarely on the side of the head. He catapulted over a pile of debris and disappeared from sight.

She retraced her steps. Gusts of wind blew her off her feet several times before she made it to the door through which she'd tried to escape before, when Squid had beaten her so seriously. Now, there was no one between her and freedom.

She reached out her hand to bang the crash bar when the door and the entire wall disappeared. The wind sucked her off her feet and she tumbled outside and across a paved parking area strewn with wreckage.

She struggled to catch her breath. She was instantly soaked. She got to her knees, gathered one foot under her, and was swept down onto the pavement again.

Suddenly, Kevin Walker was bending over her, wrestling her to her feet.

"Get me the hell out of here," she gasped.

"That's the general idea," he said.

TWO WEEKS LATER

Kevin found them sitting at a table right below the little stage used for open mic night. Dolan's Pub on Foster Street had recently re-opened after a round of renovations made necessary by the storm, and business was good.

The storm had been categorized by Environment Canada as a derecho event, much like the one that had swept through Ontario and western Quebec on May 21, 2022. That storm had been one of the worst in Canadian history, with winds up to 190 kilometers per hour, and four tornados had joined the action that day in a horrifying swath of destruction.

As for this one, while it didn't quite pile up the same statistics as its predecessor, it still caused at least $100 million in damage, and the power remained down in Perth for five days while wreckage was cleared away and repairs were made to the power distribution system throughout Lanark County.

Finally, though, the town was getting back on its feet. Businesses were re-opening, people were getting out and about again, and spirits were lifting.

They'd pushed several tables together in order to seat everyone, and they'd managed to save two places for Kevin and Janie. The crime unit was there—including Sonja, whose candy apple red Corvette had been recovered intact inside a shipping container—and so were several patrol officers, a smattering of support staff, and the detachment commander herself, who seemed to have a taste for Guinness stout. The only absentees of note were Ellie, who was recuperating at home, and Liam.

The first act was a heavy-set older man who was determined to work his way through the entire first side of *Boogie With Canned Heat*, despite the fact that almost no one in the audience knew who Canned Heat was or particularly cared. He'd brought his own karaoke tape, and while Kevin thought his harmonica playing was quite good, his attempt to duplicate the lead singer's distinctive falsetto was downright awful.

Eventually he was told to leave the stage, which he did, albeit reluctantly. He still had two more tracks to cover and felt he was just warming up.

Kevin watched in amusement as an elderly woman sat down on a stool and balanced a ventriloquist's dummy on her knee. When she began her act, she spoke in a high-pitched voice that sounded like Shirley Temple as a child, but when the dummy opened its mouth to sass her, it spoke in a remarkable contralto.

Laughing, Janie leaned over and said in his ear, "Next time I have to go in to see Brendan's teacher, I want that dummy to come with me!"

When the woman finished her act, she received an enthusiastic round of applause that seemed to fluster her. She went the wrong way to leave the stage, corrected herself, and allowed the manager to take her arm to show her to the wings.

Then it was the turn of Liam Woolfson—the reason they were all here.

He walked out onto the stage carrying a stool and a hand-held microphone. They turned a spotlight on him, and he squinted, holding up a hand.

"Now I know why John Belushi always wore sunglasses," he quipped. There was silence, and then a brief squeal of feedback. "Well, maybe it was the coke. Anyway, my name's Woolfson. Liam Woolfson. Double-five, one six nine. That's my badge number. I'm a cop."

The crowd booed—those who were paying attention.

"Now, now. Come on. We're all here to serve and protect. We've got a job to do, just like you folks. Just like the cop who pulled Schroedinger over for speeding. When he checked the trunk, he stepped back. 'Why is there a dead cat in here?' Schroedinger sighed. 'Well, sure. There is NOW.'"

The speakers hummed quietly behind him.

"I love a challenge," Liam grinned, mussing up his

dirty blond hair. "Did you here about the crook who stole a lamp? He got a very light sentence. Why did the cop arrest a turkey? Because he suspected fowl play. I like watching cop shows on TV. Like the one that has crimes committed by garden gnomes. You know, Lawn and Order."

Someone tittered. Delighted, Liam waved his hand. "There you are! I knew I'd get something for my twenty bucks!"

"When do you get funny?" someone heckled.

"Marilyn's dummy was funnier than you!" someone else added.

"You know, that dummy's not very happy. She keeps putting words in his mouth. I couldn't hear half of what he was saying. She needs to hold him closer to the mic."

Liam looked at his table of friends. Heather was laughing.

"Don't you have any jokes that aren't corny?" someone asked.

"Sorry." Liam grinned. "Say, did you hear about the ear of corn that got struck by lightning? It was shocked. What did the corn say to the man at the picnic? 'Ouch, you're biting my ear.' What does a farmer do when his corn goes on strike? Pick it."

A chorus of groans arose from the audience.

"That's all right, folks," he said. "I'll be 'ear all week." He checked his watch. "Actually, about three more minutes."

It was his biggest cheer of the night.

THREE WEEKS LATER

The Millen cottage was a comfortable four-season bungalow on Mississippi Lake near the stretch of waterfront known as Coleman's Shore. As they drove down the lane, they passed a mini-excavator parked on a spur. It was a John Deere 60G, Kevin noticed from the branding on its yellow and black body—not that it meant anything in particular to him. Just something to make a mental note of, like most other things Kevin saw around him on an average day.

As they continued into the parking area, Kevin saw that Millen hadn't bothered to remove the crime scene tape from the tool shed. He directed Constable Creed Toulouse, who was at the wheel of the Marine Unit pickup truck, to park next to it.

There were several vehicles in the yard, and over to

his left was a metal-frame gazebo. It looked as though he'd intruded on a family gathering of some sort. As he and Toulouse got out, an older man stood up, bent down to say something to the woman sitting next to him, and strolled out to meet them.

"Ed Millen?" Kevin held out his hand.

Millen stared at Kevin for a moment through his sunglasses, smoke curling around the pipe stuck in the corner of his mouth. He was a handsome devil, with a trim salt-and-pepper beard, Paul Newman lips, and muscular arms. His black golf shirt bore the logo of Millen Equipment Rentals, his former business.

"No offence," Millen said, shaking his hand, "but the wife's a little upset at another cop truck coming in here."

"None taken. It wouldn't fit in the back of my car, so I had to ask Constable Toulouse here if he could give me a hand."

"Appreciate it." Millen shook hands with Toulouse.

"Not a problem," Toulouse said. "Nice piece of machinery."

"Never laid eyes on it."

"You will now, Dad." Gerry Millen walked around the truck and leaned over the box for a look. "Looks like you guys took good care of it. I don't see no dents or scratches."

Toulouse pointed at the tool shed with his chin. "Going in there?"

"Yeah." Gerry walked over. "Okay to take this shit off?"

"I'll get it for you," Kevin said. He stripped off the crime scene tape, folded it up, and shoved it into his back pocket.

"Glad to see that gone," Ed Millen said.

Toulouse opened the door for a look. The empty space in the middle of the shed where the motor had sat was still empty.

He walked back to his truck and dropped the tailgate. The motor lay on its tiller side, the proper method to transport a four-stroke outboard. Next to it, the home-made wooden stand was also strapped down. Toulouse got busy freeing the latter.

"Christ." Ed Millen moved in for a close look. "It's a beauty, Gerry."

"Yeah."

Ed folded his arms. "I can't keep it."

"Sure you can, Dad. It's yours. Birthday and retirement present both, rolled into one."

"No," Ed shook his head, "it's not that. Every time I'd look at it I'd think of that fucking knucklehead."

"Shit. I get it. Damned fuckup."

Toulouse set up the wooden stand in the shed and came back to unstrap the motor. Kevin reached in to help out.

"You boys okay with that?" Ed asked.

"Piece of cake," Toulouse said. The motor weighed just a sliver over 360 pounds. Kevin got a solid grip on the powerhead and Toulouse grasped the midsection, just below the mounting bracket.

"Go," Kevin said.

They lifted the motor clear of the tailgate and duck-walked it over to the shed.

"Jesus," Ed said, "my back hurts just watching you guys."

Toulouse's biceps bulged and the veins in his neck stood out. Kevin concentrated on his breathing and on keeping his back straight.

They wrestled it into the shed and onto the wooden stand, then stepped back to let Gerry put a new padlock on the door.

"Thanks," Kevin said, thumping Toulouse on the shoulder.

"All in a day's work," he grinned.

There were four dedicated officers assigned to the Lanark County Marine Unit with two craft: a sixteen-foot fishing boat and a larger Boston Whaler type boat. Although they no longer conducted regular patrols, having migrated to an analytics-based policing model, officers like Toulouse were nonetheless kept busy throughout the summer with call outs as recreational boating hit full stride.

In this case, being a boating enthusiast and general busybody, Toulouse had been happy to pitch in and give Kevin a hand returning the motor to the Millens. Gerry had filled out the proper forms and obtained a release for the Merc, and Kevin had volunteered to bring it out for him. A chance conversation with Toulouse shortly thereafter had resulted in transportation and an amiable helper.

Gerry folded his arms. "Dad, what about a Yamaha?

The guy also had an F115 there. I could see if he'd swap if I pay the difference."

"Yamaha, eh?" Ed thought about it.

Toulouse grunted. "Are you talking about a 2022?"

"Yeah," Gerry said, "I think it was."

"Just so happens, that's what I've got at my cottage. Excellent motor. Not as quiet as your Merc, but completely reliable. I'm real happy with it."

"Anything's better than that damned Evinrude you got now, Dad."

Toulouse grinned. He slammed the tailgate back up and got in behind the wheel of his truck.

Ed walked with Kevin around to the passenger side. "Thanks, Walker. I appreciate the extra effort to help Gerry."

"Not a problem." They shook hands.

"He's a good man. Not like the other one."

The Crown Attorney had chosen to treat Harry Millen's theft of the outboard motor as a summary conviction offence, despite the fact that the crime was theft of property valued at over $5,000. This meant that there would be no right to trial. Harry's confession, which he made with little prompting after his arrest, along with the fact that it was his first offense and that the crime had been perpetrated against his own family, had been weighed as factors in the decision.

It would take at least eight or ten weeks before the case would be brought before a judge, but Kevin guessed that Harry would be looking at six months.

"Gerry was so upset," Ed was saying. "Giving me the damned motor was a big deal for him."

"I'm glad I was able to help."

"I owe you, buddy. I'm still plugged into the business community around here. You need something, just ask."

On the way back to Perth, Kevin mentally added Ed Millen to his growing list of informants in Lanark County.

FOUR WEEKS LATER

CHAPTER 59

After several weeks of administrative duties, Ellie was bored out of her skull. Superintendent Gavin Elliott, director of the Criminal Investigation Branch and her direct supervisor, had assigned her a mixed bag of tasks to keep her occupied while the Special Investigations Unit conducted their investigation into her use of force against Squid Navitzki. It was all dull and boring crap that she usually tried to avoid like the plague.

Gavin was her friend as well as her boss, and no doubt had her welfare in mind when he'd emptied out his Inbox into her lap, but she was less than thankful. She didn't like paperwork, she didn't like statistics, and she didn't like Human Resources junk. But she'd plowed through the stuff anyway as a favour to Gavin.

He was running a process to select an executive assistant, for example, and while HR was in charge of it, Gavin had flipped the résumés over to her for an opinion. She'd read through them, thought about it, and then sent him feedback.

The candidate she'd liked the best was a young man named Noah Mulligan. He had a degree in law, another degree in public administration, and was a former welterweight boxer who volunteered at the Royal City Boxing Club in Guelph as a coach and trainer for young people enrolled in a free program registered with Boxing Ontario. His current position, ironically enough, was administrative assistant at the Mount Forest forensic investigative facility in Wellington County. Ellie's old stomping grounds.

When she thought about the fact that she'd likely be confined to her desk until the conclusion of the SIU investigation, her heart sank. Their average length of time to close a case was currently about four months. They were chronically short-staffed, as were many other law enforcement agencies, and completion times had gotten longer as a result.

She'd been the subject of an SIU investigation before, when she'd shot and killed Rick Tassone, son of 'Ndrangheta boss Dante Tassone, during a murder investigation in Westport. The outcome of that case, though, had been expedited because of the onset of the pandemic. Now, however, she'd have to sit it out for the duration.

She understood the need for a thorough invest-igation.

Who polices the police? An age-old question. The SIU was an independent agency funded under the Ministry of the Attorney General of Ontario, and while their budget came from the AGO, they worked for the people of the province as a civilian law enforcement agency.

Their objective in each case was to determine if sufficient evidence existed in a use of force situation to charge the responsible officer with a criminal offence. In the past couple of years, an average of 3 per cent of their investigations resulted in charges.

In her situation, there were no eyewitnesses. She and Squid had been alone. She'd been through her interview and had told the unvarnished truth. The interviewer, a woman named Barbara Lévesque, took her over the incident numerous times, asking each time why, if she'd already disarmed the man, she had found it necessary to strike him a second, fatal, time.

"Section 25 of the *Code*, as you well know, Ms. March, justifies the use of force for self-defence. Once he no longer was pointing a weapon at you, though, wasn't the threat mitigated?"

Ellie thought the question was a little fatuous, given the description she'd already provided to Lévesque regarding the beating Squid had handed her earlier during her captivity, but she patiently repeated the answer she'd given several times already: "The threat presented by this individual would not be mitigated until it was completely eliminated."

"Was it your intention to kill the man?"

"No. It was my intention to end the threat."

"Are you glad you killed him?"

"No, of course I'm not."

And on it went.

The warehouse was still considered a crime scene, as investigators continued to sift through the debris for physical evidence in an attempt to compensate for a lack of witnesses. Would the thing never end?

Reggie began to bark. She went to the kitchen door, but no one was there. Neither was Reggie. He was standing at the sliding glass door to the back deck, staring at someone outside.

A man sat in one of her deck chairs, legs splayed out comfortably. She knew who it was; she'd spoken to him on the phone yesterday. He'd promised to come around for a chat.

Ellie wagged her finger at Reggie. "Friend. Lie down."

Disappointed at being relegated to the sidelines, Reggie uttered a final growl and jumped up on the couch for a nap.

Ellie made two cups of coffee, one black with honey for her and one black with nothing extra for her guest. She took them outside on a tray with an ashtray and a butane lighter.

"Hey, Chad."

The man snapped to his feet. "Let me help you with these."

He picked up a cup, sniffed, put it back down, and took his, along with the ash tray and lighter. They made themselves comfortable.

"Thanks for coming," Ellie said.

"Not at all."

When the SIU announced that the death of Squid Navitski would be investigated, Ellie's previous lawyer, Veronica Savage, had not been available, so arrangements were made for Chad Goddard to represent her. They met several times at his office in Kingston and he accompanied her to meetings and interviews with SIU investigators, but this was the first time he'd suggested getting together at her home.

She didn't know a lot about him. He liked to dress well; today it was a lightweight tan linen suit over a cream-coloured T-shirt, and chestnut slip-on loafers. His sandy hair was streaked with grey, his face was clean-shaven, and his sunglasses were stylishly expensive. He was a widower, as she understood it. A criminal attorney with experience in cases involving the *Police Services Act*.

Since Ellie's area of responsibility included Frontenac County, she'd testified twice against accused who were represented by Chad. He'd struck her as intelligent, reasonable, and polite. Respectful of her position as a commissioned officer within the OPP. He lost both cases, and took it gracefully each time. They'd gone out for coffee after the second one, and she'd found him to be a good conversationalist, relaxed and easy going. Completely professional.

He took out his cigarettes and lit one. "Business first. They finally found the chunk of two-by-four you used to take care of Squid."

"Took them long enough."

"Have mercy, Ellie. You saw the inside of that place. Some of the lumber was reduced to matchsticks. There were hundreds of pieces they had to process."

"I don't really remember what the place looked like. Anyway, they finally have their physical evidence."

"Yeah. Hopefully they'll move things along more quickly now."

"That'd be nice."

He tapped his cigarette in his ashtray. "How are you feeling?"

"Physically? Better. My ribs are still a bit sore, but I got rid of the elastic bandage a couple of days ago."

"And your nose?"

"Healing. I never had a broken nose before. I feel like a hockey player or something." She sighed. "At least I still have my front teeth."

"Your black eyes have pretty much cleared up."

She nodded. "Thank God. I looked like a raccoon."

"And emotionally?"

She took her time answering this one.

"I guess I need to talk about it."

"That's why I came down. So we could chew things over in a less formal setting."

"Still covered by confidentiality, though, right?"

He laughed. "Still covered."

She smoked, her eyes on the water. "You don't know very much about me."

"It's true; I don't."

"Not that it's important. Or germane to the investigation."

"I'll be the judge of that. Tell me about yourself."

She sighed. *What the hell.*

"I kept dreaming about Paul and Mary, my parents. More like waking dreams, I guess. I was semi-conscious, but the drugs they gave me had my brain going in a dozen different directions."

"What was it about your parents?"

"Random things." She talked about having been adopted by Paul and Mary March, Paul's parents having changed their name from Marchalewicz after moving to Canada. What it was like to grow up in their home on Yonge Street above their shoe store. She explained that only recently she'd learned that her natural parents were Jay Lippincott, a retired billionaire, and the late Juliet Magennis, a poet, office clerk, and lapsed Catholic. During Ellie's birth, a blood vessel burst and Juliet died. Unwilling to raise her, Jay had put her up for adoption, a decision he lived to regret. The whole story was something she'd never known about until a few years ago when Jay had come into her life—or *back* into her life, as it were—to attempt a reconciliation.

"You mentioned on the phone that Jay was around to see you."

"Last week, yeah."

"How did that go?"

"Good. He's a nice man."

"How does it feel to be the daughter of a billionaire?"

"It doesn't feel like anything, Chad. He has three sons, Lippincott sons, and they'll get the inheritance when Jay's gone."

"Surely you'll be included in his will?"

"I never asked. I don't really care."

"I can look into it for you."

"No." She looked around. "I'm doing just fine right here."

"That's what we need to make sure of." He stubbed out his cigarette and lit another one.

"The drugs took away my control," she finally said. "I'm a very control-oriented person, Chad. *Very*. But that was only part of the nightmare."

He kept his eyes on the water, sensing she preferred to talk without eye contact.

"I was afraid. I haven't been afraid of anything, not anything, since I was a little kid. Not even when Paul and Mary got robbed in their store. Not when I lost control of my cruiser in a snow storm and went into the ditch. Not when I faced down Rick Tassone and shot him dead. The last time I was afraid was when I wandered off down Yonge Street—I was four or five—and got lost. I remember that. But when that goddamned Squid Navitski chambered a round and pointed his Walther at me, I was afraid all over again. Just like a little girl. I thought I was going to die, and I was scared."

"Anyone would be scared," Chad ventured.

"Not me. I don't scare." She said it angrily, defiantly.

"And yet, there you were. Afraid."

She took a last pull on her cigarette and flicked it down into the tomato juice can beside her chair. "Yeah. I've been trying to ignore it, but I've got to deal with it."

"You see it as a sign of weakness."

"Damned right I do. And it started with that black Thunderbird."

"I don't quite understand."

It took her a moment to marshal her thoughts. "I had no idea the guy was going to slug me," she began. "I'm good enough at self-defence that I can usually take care of myself, but he caught me flat-footed. One in the solar plexus to paralyze me, and the other under the jaw to knock me senseless.

"They threw me in the back seat of the car they'd just stolen. A black Thunderbird. When I woke up, I was in that room. Already sedated. It felt like I'd been transported in a vintage black hearse to some way station on the road to Purgatory."

"That's very medieval."

"Yeah, I guess so. But that's when the fear started. I hid it from them because once they know you're afraid, it's game over. But the drugs lowered my defences, and I couldn't help it. I kept lying there, thinking back to things in my past, my failures and, I don't know, rookie mistakes."

"You don't need to be so hard on yourself, Ellie. You're one of the finest law enforcement professionals it's been my privilege to know."

"Thanks. I'll tell you one thing, though. When they told

me the gang had chopped that damned Thunderbird up into parts, I felt like throwing a party. My damned black hearse. Nothing left but a carburetor, a transmission, leather seats, and a metal cube the size of a microwave oven. I guess they figured it was the safer way to go. Generally speaking, they were a very risk-averse bunch. Bruno in particular."

She stood up, coffee cup in hand. "I'm going to put a stick in this. How about you?"

Chad shook his head as he passed his cup over. "I'm driving, but another coffee would be great."

In the kitchen, as she waited for the coffee machine to do its thing, she grabbed the bottle of Jack Daniel's from the cupboard and took a swig. When her coffee was ready, she added a dollop to it, a tear running down her cheek.

Back outside, she lit another cigarette. "My mind kept going back to my first homicide case as a detective constable. A guy named Leif Brand was my mentor. Babysitter. In Wellington County. A lot of what I know is thanks to him. I miss the guy."

"Is he still there? In Wellington?"

She shook her head. "Brain tumour. Killed him three months after he found out. I was in Orillia at the time, but I made it to his funeral."

"My condolences."

"Leif was solid as a rock. It was a bad case. A girl thrown off a cliff. The animals had worked on her pretty good before parts of her began to turn up the next day."

"It sounds pretty horrific."

"Anyway, I learned a lot from that case. It was my first

one, and it was the making of me."

"Probably you kept thinking about it because it reminded you of who you are. *What* you are."

She said nothing for a moment, lost in thought.

"I remember that case," he said. "I remember the Manitoba one more clearly, of course, because it was so horrible and was sensationalized by the press. Gerald Alcorn and Anna Leigh Dombrowski. But I do recall her having turned up in Guelph, years later, but I don't remember the outcome."

"She got off. She told me she would, when I arrested her, and she was right. The Crown Attorney kept saying, 'Get more evidence, get more evidence,' but it just wasn't there to be gotten. Our best interrogator, Jim Waterfield, tried to break her down in interrogation, but she was too good. She stuck to her guns and refused to confess. That was it. She walked."

"She disappeared again, didn't she?"

"Yeah. I never found out where she went." Ellie grimaced. "We talked to Cindy's friend Madison again, and found out that Cindy had told her she'd learned something about her ex-step-mother that she was going to hold over her head. Brand figured she'd somehow learned about Dawn's real identity and tried to extort money from her. God only knows why Madison hadn't mentioned that to us before, but there you go.

"Dawn would have driven to the house that Saturday to have it out with the girl and ended up driving her to the hiking trail to dispatch her once and for all. Which would explain the evidence of strangulation at the top of the cliff. But we could never prove it."

"And what about your kidnappers? Will you guys be able to track them down?"

Ellie snorted. "I'd love to arrest their asses, that's for sure, and see them go off to prison. They took off during the storm, and they could have ended up anywhere."

"Montreal?"

"Maybe. There's a JFO working on it. We'll see if they turn up anything. They're probably out of the country by now, though. Bruno especially. Their big boss, Leonardo Arcuri, has also ghosted."

"There were fatalities."

She shrugged. "Yeah. Junior Paul, for one. Killed by debris while trying to escape. A mechanic I never met was crushed by a flying car. And Squid Navitski." She touched her nose gingerly. "I hit that bastard as hard as I could, Chad."

"I understand."

She shook her head, watching the whitecaps out on the lake, flipped up by passing gusts of wind. "You're discreet, Chad. I'll give you that."

"I may be Catholic," he said, "but I'm no priest. I can't take your confession and offer you forgiveness from God. Anyway, you're not a baptized Catholic, so I couldn't even if I wanted to."

"Actually, I am."

Chad looked surprised. "Oh? Is that true?"

"Jay told me. Like I said, my mother was a lapsed

Catholic, but the day before I was born, she told Jay she wanted me baptized. So before I went up for adoption, he had it done himself. Jay Lippincott in a Catholic church with little me, getting splashed with holy water. Feature that."

"I actually know something about this," Chad said. "It's called a 'founded hope' baptism. It came up in one of my cases. The priest believes there is a founded hope that the child would be raised as a Catholic. Your father may have said he'd pass along this 'hope' to the adoption agency."

"Guess it didn't take, though. Here I am, a heathen agnostic."

"But there's still hope that some day you'll change your mind?"

She sighed at him. "I don't know, Chad. That's not a question I can answer right now."

"Fair enough." He waited, but she was done.

"How soon would you like to return to your regular duties, Ellie?"

"Yesterday."

"Do you think you're ready for it?"

"I was born ready for it."

"Do you want me to have a word with Gavin Elliott?"

"No. That's a call I need to make myself."

"As you wish, Ellie. As you wish."

"Very funny, Chad." She bit her lip. "What happens if they decide to lay charges against me?"

"We'll make sure that doesn't happen."

"But what if it does? What the hell will I do?"

"We'll fight them, Ellie. But let's cross that bridge if we get to it."

"I'll have to resign my commission. Especially if I'm convicted. Maybe even if I'm not. My career will be over."

"We won't let it get that far," he said.

She made a fist and tapped it lightly on the arm of her chair.

Chad took out his cigarettes and lit another. "There's another reason I came up here today."

"Why am I not surprised."

"No, no, no," he said in mock horror, "don't you misunderstand me. I came up to see you, first and foremost. An indulgent pleasure, eh?"

"Bullshit."

"Not at all. But look, I also came up to see the lake."

"Nice, isn't it?"

"Do you actually like it here?"

She frowned. "Yes, of course I do. Very quiet. The neighbours are good."

"You don't have any plans to move in the next while?"

"Nope. I'm burrowed in here like a tick in Reggie's fur. Speaking of which, I've got some stuff I have to remember to give him for that."

Chad leaned back in his chair and crossed his legs. "I've done some research. Sparrow Lake is part of the Gananoque River watershed. Over thirteen kilometers of shoreline. Maximum depth of four and a half meters, give or take. No invasive species to worry about. Good fishing. I like to fish. Pike, bass, brown bullheads. Blackened Cajun-style catfish is one of my go-to specialties."

"I didn't know any of this."

"It's a good lake." He smiled at her. "The reason for my curiosity is that a cousin of mine owns a four-season here. On the other side, up on Treetop Lane."

"Ah. I see." She thought for a moment. She'd kept up to date on the other property owners on the lake, as a precautionary measure against suspicious activity that might have an impact on her own use of the cottage as a remote workplace. She ran Treetop through her memory. There were no Goddards. "Webster? Or Hudson?"

He laughed. "Scotty Webster. Yes. Do you know him?"

"No. We've never met. I just know of him."

"He's older than I am. He and his wife have lived on the lake for nearly ten years, but they've decided to sell it and buy one of those new waterfront condos in Brockville."

Ellie thought the light was beginning to dawn. "And you're considering taking it off his hands. Investment property?"

"I suppose," he conceded. "Property values haven't exactly gone down around here, that's for sure."

"Would you rent it out?" Ellie didn't like the thought; renters with noisy boats and poor littering habits would not be welcomed by her neighbours—nor by herself, when it came right down to it.

But Chad was shaking his head. "For my own personal use. It only takes an hour to get here from my house, which seems fine to me. It would be nice to be able to get away from the city on weekends, and for a week or two during the holidays. It's so nice here."

Ellie said nothing, thinking about it. Would it be a good idea to have her attorney so close by? Would he encroach on her privacy? Would she be obligated to socialize with him? Would he want to discuss the case against her at times when she just wanted to block it out and think about other things?

Chad watched these thoughts pass across her face as clearly as though he could read her mind. "Oh, dear. Oh, dear. I'm sorry, Ellie. I've made a mistake."

"A mistake?"

"I thought, well, I thought I might . . ."

Ellie stared at him. He was crushed. She was missing something. She watched him stub out his cigarette and stand up.

"Thanks for the coffee. I'll let you know as soon as I hear something more from the investigators."

She stopped him with her hand. "Chad, what is it? Did I say something wrong?"

"No, of course not. I should get going. Scotty's expecting me." He frowned. "I'll tell him just to go ahead and put it on the market."

Ellie was thoroughly confused. "I thought you were interested in it."

"It was a mistake. Don't worry about it."

Her hand was still on his arm. He took her wrist, gently, and lifted it clear.

In that moment, she understood.

"Oh, my god."

He started to laugh. "Christ, I'm caught."

"You're not—you're not—"

"Interested in you? What the hell gave you that idea? Me falling all over myself like an adolescent fool? Was that the first clue?"

"Sit. Sit down. Don't go yet. Sit."

"No, thanks. I really should get going."

She stood up. "For godsakes, don't let me stop you from buying that cottage if you really want it."

He smiled. "Ellie, there are dozens of cottages for sale within a half an hour of Kingston. There's only one reason why I'd buy this one."

She didn't know what to say.

"We've been negotiating a number. I'll see if it's worth what he wants for it." He leaned down and kissed her on the cheek. "May I call you tomorrow?"

"Yes. Please do."

She stood there, listening to the sound of his car leaving her parking spot and easing back up the lane to the road that would take him around to the other side of the lake. When there was nothing else to hear but the wind coming off the water and sifting through the boughs of the evergreens, she went back inside.

She made a fresh cup of coffee, without the Jack Daniels this time, and went back out, stepping aside to let Reggie barge past her. He hunted around for Chad's scent, and once he was satisfied that the interloper was gone, he trotted down the stairs to do his rounds.

Ellie sat down. Her body still felt beat up and wrecked. She had a dozen different aches and pains to remind her of her ordeal. She'd passed up on the prescription medications they'd offered her and was determined to fight it out, but the healing process was taking longer than she wished.

Mentally, it was pretty much the same. She still had the odd nightmare about fists and boots striking her from out of nowhere, but soon they'd go away. She hoped.

She put all that aside and thought about Chad. She pictured the map of the lake in her mind, and she knew which property belonged to Webster. She got up and walked down to the dock. Reggie followed her down to the end. He looked up at her, seemed to mentally shrug, and jumped in.

She watched him paddle around, enjoying the swim, before heading back to shore. When the water was ankle-deep, he shook himself vigorously and ran up onto the deck.

Wet, stinky dog.

Just the kind she loved.

She looked down the lake in the direction of the Webster place, but couldn't see it from here. Just as well, she supposed.

She joined Reggie on the deck. Leaning back in the chair, she closed her eyes.

Very seldom had a man expressed an interest in her. The last to do so was Danny Merrick, an RCMP assistant commissioner who was on a long-term assignment in Brussels. They'd had a bit of a fling, but with his prolonged absence it had evolved into a long-term friendship rather than a romance. When he'd called last November to tell her he was getting married to a Belgian woman and wouldn't be back to Canada for a while, they'd agreed it would be best not to communicate further going forward.

Ellie wasn't particularly upset. She was a lone wolf, after all, and she valued her solitude.

Now, however, she felt as though the ordeal Bruno and his crew had put her through had punctured the shell she'd built around herself and introduced feelings of vulnerability she'd rather not be experiencing right now.

Shit. What a load of crap.

Chad Goddard was handsome, kind, and intelligent. And interested. Only a few years younger. What the hell was wrong with her?

This was Eleanor March at fifty-one years of age.

Oxford Station, Ontario
August 3, 2025

ACKNOWLEDGMENTS

As always, it's important to bear in mind that this novel is a work of fiction, and while the Ontario Provincial Police is an actual law enforcement entity, all characters are entirely the product of my imagination, as are the situations in which they find themselves and the things they do as a result. Any variations from OPP policies, procedures, or legislative authorities are the product of my active imagination or are errors or misinterpretations for which I apologize.

Information related to animal scavenging may be found in *Taphonomic Signatures of Animal Scavenging in Northern California: A Forensic Anthropological Analysis*, A Thesis by Lisa N. Bright. Spring 2011, California State University, Chico; Master of Arts in Biology. scholarworks.calstate.edu/concern/theses/xw42n8523, viewed February 21, 2025.

Further information on animal scavenging may be found in Jarrett Hallcox and Amy Welch. *Bodies We've Buried* (New York: The Berkeley Publishing Group, 2006), p. 97.

Insight into the state of footprint and tire tread analysis in 2002 may be found in Sauerwein, K. (2024) "Summary of Published Criticisms of Footwear and Tire Impression Examination and Responses." (National Institute of Standards and Technology, Gaithersburg, MD), NIST Interagency Report (IR) NIST IR 8509sup2. http://doi.

org/10.6028/NIST.IR.8509sup 2, viewed June 28, 2025.

To learn more about the Special Investigations Unit, consult their *Annual Report 2023-2024*, siu.on.ca/en/annual_report_2023.php, p. 31, accessed June 4, 2025.

Liam Woolfson owes a debt of thanks to *Homer and Jethro's "Cornfucius Say" Joke Book*, (Kellogg's Corn Flakes, 1964; public domain) for some of his cornier material. Yes, my mom sent away for this for me when I saw it advertised on the back of a Corn Flakes box. I was nine. That's not an excuse, just an explanation. She regretted the kindness thereafter, but I've always treasured this little jewel.

Information on interrogation techniques came from two sources: Frank J. MacHovic, *Interview and Interrogation: A Scientific Approach* (Springfield, Ill.: Charles C. Thomas Publications Ltd., 1989); and Kassin, Saul M., Sara C. Appleby and Jennifer Torkildson Perillo, "Interviewing suspects: Practice, science, and future directions," *Legal and Criminological Psychology*, The British Psychological Society, 2009, which considered the Reid Technique and its shortcomings.

Finally, as always, it behooves me to acknowledge the patience, tolerance, guidance, and endless support from which I've benefited once again as the spouse of Lynn L. Clark—my editor, best friend, and life partner.

About the Author

Michael J. McCann lives and writes
in Oxford Station, Ontario, Canada. A
graduate of Trent University (Peterborough, ON) and Queen's University
(Kingston, ON), he served as Production
Editor of *Criminal Reports (Third Series)*
and Law Reports Co-ordinator for Carswell
Legal Publications (Western) before
spending fifteen years at the Canada Border
Services Agency as a project officer and
national program manager. He's married to
author Lynn L. Clark. They have one son,
Tim McCann.

Finalist for the
HAMMETT PRIZE
for
Best Crime Novel in North America

Sorrow Lake
March and Walker #1

Michael J. McCann
ISBN: 978-1-927884-02-7

Ask your local independent bookstore
to order it today!

www.ingramcontent.com/pod-product-compliance
Lightning Source LLC
Chambersburg PA
CBHW022005050726
47499CB00002BA/305